Dan Rhodes has written eight other books and won a bunch of prizes, including the E. M. Forster Award. He lives in Derbyshire.

www.danrhodes.co.uk

Also by Dan Rhodes:

Anthropology and a Hundred Other Stories
Don't Tell me the Truth about Love
Timoleon Vieta Come Home
The Little White Car
Gold
Little Hands Clapping
This is Life
Marry Me

When the Professor Got Stuck in the Snow

AARDVARK
BUREAU

When the Professor Got Stuck in the Snow

Dan Rhodes

Aardvark Bureau
London

An Aardvark Bureau Book
An imprint of Gallic Books

First published by Miyuki Books in 2014
Copyright © Dan Rhodes, 2014
Dan Rhodes asserts his moral right to be identified
as the author of this work.

This edition published in Great Britain in 2015 by
Aardvark Bureau, 59 Ebury Street, London, SW1W 0NZ

A CIP record for this book is available from the British Library

ISBN 978-1-910709-01-6

Typeset in Caslon Pro by Aardvark Bureau
Printed in the UK by CPI (CR0 4YY)
2 4 6 8 10 9 7 5 3

For Wife-features, Arthur & Eddie

Thursday, 28th November 2013

1

Two men were sitting opposite one another in an otherwise empty railway carriage. The first was hidden behind a large newspaper while the second, a man of indeterminate age who went by the name of Smee, looked out at the landscape as the train made its way through the countryside. The carriage was warm, but the trees were bare, and ponds were freezing over. Ducks could be seen walking on water. *I wonder if it will begin to snow*, thought Smee. *It certainly seems cold enough.*

This moment of idle conjecture was brought to an end by a series of snorts from behind the newspaper, followed by a 'Ptchwwfffff'. The paper was folded, to reveal an exasperated face. 'Take a letter for me, Smee.'

'Certainly, Professor.'

Smee opened his computer. His fingers hovered over the keyboard, waiting for the words to flow.

After a little academic chin-stroking, the Professor began. 'To the editor of the *Daily Telegraph* of London: Sir, I find it quite extraordinary that you have allowed your newspaper to be used as a forum for the propagation of poppycock. Today you published an article by Justin Welby, the – quotes – Archbishop of

Canterbury – close quotes – in which he discusses his – quotes – faith – close quotes. This is a man whose entire life revolves around his belief in fairy stories. If this piece had appeared on your world-renowned Funnies Page it would have been in some way understandable, but to treat it as serious comment defies common sense. You might as well have told your readers that there is a goblin with a purple face. With all best wishes, Richard Dawkins – brackets – Professor – exclamation mark – exclamation mark – exclamation mark – exclamation mark ...' The Professor thought for a while longer. 'Exclamation mark. How many exclamation marks are we up to, Smee?'

Smee counted. 'That would be five, Professor.'

'Hmmm ... Four would not be quite enough, and six excessive. I am resolute that five is the correct amount for the circumstances. Close brackets. The end. Put it in one of those email things of yours and send it off, would you?'

'Certainly, Professor,' said Smee. *What a mind*, he thought, as he went back over his typing to smooth out the punctuation and make sure his fingers had not, in their excitement, made any mistakes. *What a brilliant mind.*

The Professor closed his eyes and began to make having-a-nap sounds, and with each man occupied in his own way neither noticed the first snow begin to fall. It was powdery, hardly snow at all, but before long the flakes were coming down large and thick, and there was no getting away from it.

Winter had arrived.

2

The train juddered to a stop, rousing the Professor.

'What is the meaning of this?' he thundered, as he typically did upon being woken from a nap. He blinked for a while, until the world came into focus and he deduced the root of the problem. 'Ptchah. One little snow flurry and the country grinds to a halt.'

Smee pulled an expression that indicated agreement with the Professor's comment. It was an expression he had been using a lot.

'Remind me, Smee,' said the Professor, 'where are we going?'

Smee checked his notes. 'Upper Bottom, Professor, where you are due to give a talk at the village hall to the All Bottoms Women's Institute on the subject of "Science and the non-existence of God". It's not until tomorrow afternoon, so I'm sure we'll get there on time.' As Smee spoke, he wondered where this confidence had come from. Far from being one little flurry, the snow was now so thick that the landscape had all but vanished; a strong wind was blowing, and already it was starting to drift.

The public address system clicked into life and a voice filled the carriage: '*Dmmf a vmmph whmpf crumph a sthmph wpff tmphf mmpff hmpff.*'

'Are we in Wales, Smee?'

'No, Professor, we are in the very heart of the English countryside.'

'Then why is the conductor speaking in Welsh? Proud language as it is, it hardly seems appropriate.'

'It wasn't Welsh, Professor; it was just a rather fuzzy-sounding announcement.'

'Are you telling me that was supposed to be Her Majesty's English?' he raged. 'It was an inaudible disgrace. I shall be writing one of my letters about this. Could you understand a word of it?'

Smee had an uncommon talent for deciphering railway announcements. 'Due to adverse weather conditions,' he said, 'this service will terminate at Market Horten.'

'Market Horten? Phmph. I've never heard of it.'

Smee hadn't either. He opened his computer and was relieved to find a faint signal. He tapped away for a while and extracted the required knowledge. 'It's a town a few miles down the line from where we are now. Population six thousand.'

'Is it close to where I am due to give my talk?'

Smee again referred to his computer, looking at a map of the cluster of villages that made up the Bottoms. 'Market Horten is described as being "the Gateway to the Bottoms", but I'm afraid it's still some way away. Lower Bottom is the nearest of the Bottoms, and that's around three miles from town. Then you have East Bottom and West Bottom, with Middle Bottom in between; then comes Inner Bottom, followed by Great Bottom, and our destination is a full eleven miles from Market Horten. It's looking rather unlikely that we shall be able to reach Upper Bottom tonight.'

'But we must reach Upper Bottom, by hook or by crook. That is a shepherd's crook, you understand, not a bishop's crook. I have women to speak to tomorrow afternoon, many of whom will be deluded churchgoers who urgently need to hear the truth about religion from somebody who has done all the experiments.'

'If the snow eases, the rail service might resume by the morning,' said Smee, at once hopeful and hopeless.

As they sat immobile, the snow showed no sign of easing. 'Pfff ...' said the Professor, looking at his watch. 'There goes *Deal or No Deal*.'

When, at last, the train lurched back to life and started to move slowly towards what would now be its final stop, there was little daylight left and Smee knew in his heart that they would have to find shelter for the night in the small town of Market Horten.

He went back online to find out what he could about their temporary home. He made a telephone call, and before the train had reached the station he had arranged for them to be met there by a taxi driver called Dave, who would help them find accommodation.

The Professor took this news with interest. 'Imagine me, Professor Richard Dawkins, consorting with a taxi driver named *Dave*. Remember this, Smee, and if anybody puts it to you that I keep only elite company, and that I am out of touch with the common man, you be sure to tell them about the time we spent with Dave the taxi driver from ... Where are we again?'

3

The Professor and Smee were bundled up in overcoats and scarves, but even so they shivered as they waited in the dim light of the small shelter outside Market Horten's two-platform railway station. Smee wished he had worn an extra pair of socks.

The snow was swirling around them and blowing into high drifts. Some parked cars were completely buried. 'This is some pretty bad weather, Professor,' said Smee, at once regretting having spoken.

'*Some pretty bad weather?* Listen to yourself, Smee. Try again.'

Smee was disappointed in himself. He thought for a moment. 'The meteorological conditions are somewhat inclement, Professor.'

'That's more like it. There remains room for improvement, but progress has been made.'

They didn't have to wait long before a light grey car approached, making tracks through the snow. As it neared them, large blue letters on the side were revealed: 'Dave's Taxi'.

'You do the talking, Smee.'

'Of course, Professor.'

'Evening, boys,' said Dave in his mild rural accent. Leaving the car running, he opened the boot and put their four heavy cases in. Smee sat in the front, and the Professor in the back. Dave got in. 'Interesting journey, boys?' he asked.

'You might say that,' said Smee. 'Now, I wonder if you would be able to find us something in the way of accommodation?'

'It's a bit tricky at this time of year,' said Dave, carefully pulling away. 'Most places round here close for the winter, but I've made a phone call or two and found you a room. There's a nice old couple that does a bit of B&B in the summer, and they've agreed to take you boys in, even though they're shut. They said they couldn't have you freezing on the streets.'

'Splendid,' said Smee. 'Thank you. Did you discuss with them the small matter of recompense?'

'Er ... what?'

'Did they give you any indication of how their out-of-season tariff might impact upon our budget?'

'Eh?'

'How much will it cost?'

'Oh, nothing. They're putting you up for free. Wayfarers caught in the snow, and all that. We're like that round here, boys, I'm afraid.'

'That is ever so good of them.' Smee felt the inevitable response at being the object of kindness: warmth coursed through his body.

The taxi moved slowly through the snow.

'I'll be off home after this,' said Dave. 'Back to the

wife and three. Even with my winter tyres on I won't be able to keep going much longer.' His was the last car on the road.

From the back seat the Professor spoke to Smee. 'Ask him about the chances of me reaching Upper Bottom.'

Smee had become quite used to the Professor's aversion to small talk, and his reluctance to engage in direct conversation unless it was within the context of a professional engagement or fevered debate. Before he could ask the question, Dave, having heard everything, answered.

'That depends on the weather. I hear the Bottoms are blocked. If this white stuff keeps coming I can't see that changing.'

'Ask him if there's a local helicopter we can commandeer. This is something of an emergency: I have an important talk to give.'

'We ain't got no 'copter, boy, but we might be able to load you into a trailer and pull you up there behind a tractor. But even that's not looking likely. There's some big hills between here and there, and the snow could be six foot deep by the morning.'

'We shall get there somehow, Smee. On horseback, if necessary.'

Dave was thoughtful for a moment. 'Upper Bottom, you say? Giving a talk?'

Smee answered on the Professor's behalf. 'Yes, the Professor is due to address the All Bottoms Women's Institute tomorrow afternoon.'

Dave craned his neck and looked in the rear-view mirror. 'Prod me with a parsnip! It's him, isn't it? It's Professor Dawkins.'

'The very same,' said Smee.

'Well, now, it's an honour to have him in my taxi. I saw a poster for his talk when I was taking Old Aggie up the Bottoms the other day. I thought about going myself, but it's the WI isn't it? They wouldn't let me in unless I was wearing a dress.' Dave chuckled at his joke, and even Smee smiled a little. Only the Professor remained stony-faced, making it clear that to him this was no laughing matter. 'I happen to have read your books,' said Dave.

'Do you really think he has read my books, Smee? A simple taxi driver from the countryside? A taxi driver named *Dave*?'

'Oh yes, I've read 'em alright, boy. Actually I'd better not call you boy, had I? I'll call you "Prof" from now on.'

'Ask him what he thought of *The Extended Phenotype*, Smee. I have always had a soft spot for that one, you know.'

'Well, I've not actually read that one,' said Dave.

'Then perhaps *River Out of Eden*?'

'Er, no, I've not read that one neither, I'm afraid.'

'I wonder which ones he *has* read.'

'The one about genes, and the God one. Interesting stuff, Prof.'

'Obvious choices, Smee, but it is still rather heart-warming to hear that my work, albeit the more populist end of my output, has touched the life of somebody as humdrum as this Dave character.'

'I am pretty humdrum, you're not wrong there,' said Dave, cheerfully, 'but I do like a bit of a read on the rank from time to time. Now then, here we are.'

They pulled up outside a small stone house with the ghost of roses around the door. The front path had been shovelled clear and gritted, ready for their arrival.

'Nice people,' said Dave, as he opened the boot of the taxi and took out half of the men's luggage. 'He's a retired vicar, and she's a retired vicar's wife.' Dave carried the bags up to the door of the house, leaving the men to get out of the car in their own time.

'Christians, Smee,' said the Professor, looking straight ahead, his eyes glinting, alive with the possibilities that lay ahead. He even smiled a little. 'Christians! Let us remember my motto.'

'There is no God.'

'No, not that one, the other one.'

'I am the expert.'

'No, no, one of my other ones: Cordiality always.'

'Of course, Professor. Cordiality always.' Smee had never heard him use this motto before. He was sure he would apply it though. The Professor would be as civil as it was possible to be as he made mincemeat of their elderly hosts. And he would have a ringside seat.

This was the stuff of dreams.

4

It was Mrs Potter who answered the door, all silver bun and smiles. 'Hello Dave,' she said.

'You'll never believe who I've brought you today, Mrs P.,' said Dave. 'You could have bopped me with a beetroot when I recognised him. It's only that science bloke, Professor Richard Dawkins.'

'Oh dear,' said Mrs Potter, flustered. 'I'm afraid I don't think we ought to have agreed to this. If I had known it was him, I would have had to say no.'

'What's the problem, Mrs P.?' asked Dave. 'I thought you were the open-minded type.'

'I am, Dave, it's just the practicalities. This is a very old house, and it really wasn't designed with wheelchairs in mind. I would hate for him to be uncomfortable. He'll have to go up half a dozen steps if he needs to spend a penny in the night. He has to sleep somewhere though; let me think where else we could try for the poor man …'

'Wheelchairs? What are you …?' The penny dropped. 'No, Mrs P., it's not him – it's the other one.'

'The other one? I didn't realise there *was* another one.'

'You're thinking of the space one. This one's Richard Dawkins, the one who's really into his genomes. He can't get enough of them; he's even been on BBC2 talking about them.'

'Oh, I don't know,' said Mrs Potter, turning red. 'Me and my mistakes.'

Reverend Potter appeared, his remaining hair just as white as the world outside. 'Hello Dave. Are they here?' he asked.

'They certainly are. And – touch me with a turnip – it's only that scientist Professor Dawkins, and some other bloke – his male secretary, I suppose. Nice enough pair of lads, anyway, just a bit weird – but you'd expect that from people like them, wouldn't you?'

'How exciting,' said the Reverend. 'I do hope I shall be able to have a little chat with him over supper. He seems like a jolly interesting fellow. Will you show them in, Dave?'

Mrs Potter scuttled off to make some final preparations to their room, and the vicar heartily greeted the men as they crunched their way up the garden path. At the door Smee discreetly settled up with Dave as he brought in their remaining bags. It had been a short journey, and the meter had only read four pounds sixty, but he pressed a twenty-pound note into Dave's hand in a way that made it clear that no change was required and nothing needed to be said. Dave had, after all, been extremely helpful and would be out of work until the snow cleared up. He hoped the Professor wouldn't notice him doing this. 'Never tip taxi drivers, Smee,' he had said on a number of occasions. 'It only encourages them.'

As the son of a taxi driver, whose annual family trip

to the seaside had been paid for out of the tip jar, Smee couldn't bring himself to leave a decent cabbie without a little on top of the fare. This rare insubordination had to take place in the shadows, and Dave stuck to the script with a valedictory 'Much obliged'.

On their first meeting the Professor had explained that he had been having some difficulties while his local branch of Lloyds Bank turned into a TSB, so it had been down to Smee to cover their day-to-day expenses. Smee didn't have the opportunity to ask for a receipt from Dave though, so he knew he wouldn't be seeing the money again. Still, he was pleased to have got away with leaving a tip, and with that behind him he allowed himself to be ushered alongside the Professor into the warmth of the sitting room, where a log fire blazed.

'Welcome, Professor Dawkins,' the Reverend said, extending his hand. 'What an honour to have you under our roof.'

'Yes, yes, of course.' The Professor shook the vicar's hand in a businesslike manner.

The Reverend turned to Smee. 'And welcome to you too, Mr ...'

'He is my male secretary,' said the Professor, 'and his name is Smee.'

'Is that *Mr* Smee, or Smee *something*?'

'Just Smee,' answered the Professor on Smee's behalf.

Smee had become quite used to his new name, and liked that it stood alone. On their first meeting the Professor had looked him up and down and said, 'Henceforth you shall answer to *Smee,*' and Smee couldn't think of a single reason why he would not be happy about this.

'How unusual,' said the vicar. 'If you have no objection I shall pour you each a brandy and leave you to thaw out while I nip off to see if my wife has finished preparing your room. I wonder, would you condescend to join us for a rather humble meal this evening?'

'That would be very kind,' said Smee, who was ravenous. 'Thank you.' As soon as he said this, he realised his mistake: he should have waited for the Professor to answer, and then followed his lead. It was too late now.

The Professor must have known that they would be hard pressed to find succour elsewhere on a night like this. He forced his lips into a smile. 'How nice,' he said.

'Do you see how cordial I can be?' said the Professor, when the Reverend had left the room. 'Even when confronted with the very worst kind of reckless imbecile I shake hands and smile and so forth. Cordiality always.'

'You are an inspiration, Professor.'

'You're not wrong there, Smee.'

The men stood near the fire, sipping their brandies. Following his earlier indiscretion, Smee made a point of not speaking unless spoken to, and for several minutes the Professor said nothing. Eventually, though, he broke the silence by looking disdainfully at his brandy glass, and saying, 'Supermarket rubbish.'

Smee, who had been greatly enjoying his brandy until

that moment, elected to remain silent, but once again he found himself pulling a face that signalled agreement.

Mrs Potter came into the room and introduced herself to her guests. 'Could I show you to your room, gentlemen?' she asked. 'I hope you don't mind sharing, but I'm afraid it's the only one we could possibly prepare at such short notice.'

'Needs must when the Devil drives,' said the Professor, as they followed Mrs Potter out of the room. 'I mean that as a figure of speech,' he explained to Smee, clearly aware that Mrs Potter was within earshot. 'Of course there is no such thing as the Devil; that would be preposterous.'

They went upstairs and into a small room with twin beds. Nearly everything about it was just as would be expected from a country bed and breakfast. It was simply decked out, with dark wooden furniture and watercolours of rural scenes. There was, though, one unusual aspect to it.

'What is the meaning of this?' bellowed the Professor, pointing at a garden gnome on a bedside table, blank eyes staring from a cheerful face. 'And this?' He had noticed another. 'And this?' One by one he pointed at gnome after gnome, until a dozen were accounted for. All cordiality had drained from him.

'Oh dear,' said Mrs Potter. 'I seem to have made one of my mistakes. Dave told me you were a big fan of G-gnomes, and I thought you might appreciate us putting our collection in your room, to make you feel at home. We've brought them in for the winter, you see, and I thought I would get them out of the cupboard and put them on display. It's my mistake; I should have known that our little garden gnomes might not be up to scratch. Do they not meet your exacting standards, Professor?'

'G-gnomes, you say?' The fury on his face melted away. 'Of course.' He looked again at the gnomes. 'Well, yes, I am rather taken with them, as it goes. Not bad specimens, all told. They are rather jolly little chaps, aren't they? They will do.'

Mrs Potter was relieved with this outcome. 'Oh, I'm so glad,' she said. 'I was starting to think I had made another of my mistakes.' She bustled around, telling them where the kettle was, and showing how the curtains worked, and giving directions to the bathroom. 'We eat at seven, gentlemen. I look forward to you joining us.'

She left them alone, to make themselves comfortable.

'That was what is scientifically known as "a mildly amusing misunderstanding", Smee,' said the Professor.

'Yes, Professor,' said Smee.

'But it is over now. We shall think of it no more, except perhaps to recall my jovial response to the episode when next I am wrongly accused of lacking a sense of whimsy.'

For a moment Smee couldn't wait to recount the story to somebody, but it hit him that there was nobody. Nobody at all. He had only the Professor now.

5

With an hour to fill before their meal, the men settled into their room, emptying cases and filling drawers. The Professor tutted when it became clear that there were no complimentary biscuits.

Smee felt his days were full of purpose now, as he dealt with the logistics of an extended tour of Britain. There had been much to overcome, but at that moment he was more relieved than ever: he had conquered the blizzard and seen to it that the Professor had a warm bed for the night.

'What is your opinion of our hosts, Smee?' asked the Professor, as he separated his pH paper into colour-coded stacks.

Smee knew that the Professor would scrutinise his answer, and he hoped he would say the right thing. His heart raced. 'They are a pair of idiots,' he said, 'just like anybody who believes in all that superstitious nonsense.' He could sense that the Professor was approving so far, and he carried on. 'They are a throwback to the Dark Ages. But at least their stupidity manifests itself in some small degree of kindness; it was, I suppose, good of them to take us in.'

Smee wished he had finished with them being a

throwback to the Dark Ages. He could sense that this last comment had not met the Professor's approval.

'*Kindness*?' said the Professor. '*Good of them*? Smee, what are you thinking? Have you learned nothing from me? Their kindness is as hollow as an eggshell. An empty eggshell, that is to say. They are only being kind in the hope that God sees them and gives them a pat on the back for it when they get to heaven. Well, let me tell you this, Smee,' he roared. 'There is no God and there is no heaven. I am disappointed in you. True kindness can only ever come from Humanists such as myself, we who know that there is nothing waiting for us when we die, nothing but decomposition and dissipation and that sort of thing. Unlike Christians, we don't go around being kind in the hope of collecting heaven points. Do you think I am kind, Smee?' His eyes narrowed. 'Well, do you?'

Smee was desperate to make up lost ground. 'You are *very* kind, Professor.'

'You are quite right. I have devoted swathes of my life to kindly telling people how ignorant they are, and correcting them, and giving them the opportunity to think as I do. Look at me now, traipsing through the countryside, taking only modest fees, sometimes no fee at all, as I inform the clueless that there is no God, just as there is no goblin with a purple face, and that there is no consolation, none whatsoever, to be found in religion. If anybody is kind around here, Smee, it is me – and I am unanimous in that.'

'Yes, Professor.'

'Hmph. You keep quiet and think about what you said while I call my third wife. She worries so.' The Professor pulled out his old-fashioned mobile phone and dialled. 'Hello dear. Yes, there has been a bit of snow, but I've been taken in by some Creationist halfwits so at least I have a bed for the night. Yes, it is warm indoors. Yes, I do have a change of underwear.'

There was a knock at the door. Smee answered, and in walked Mrs Potter. 'I'm terribly sorry,' she said, 'but I had completely forgotten to leave towels out for you.'

The Professor continued talking. 'So here I am, trapped for the time being … What's that, dear? Why no, your ears are not deceiving you; there is a woman in here with me, but that is not your concern. Right now I have just one ambition in life, and that is to see Upper Bottom. Only when I have achieved this shall I be satisfied.'

Having placed a towel at the foot of each bed, Mrs Potter left the room.

The Professor looked at his phone. 'That was rather odd, Smee. My third wife seemed to be suddenly cut off. There was a loud clunk, and then nothing. Probably the meteorological conditions, Smee. Yes, that'll be it. There is no mystery. See – there is a scientific explanation for everything.'

6

'I know it's not really your thing, Professor,' said the Reverend Potter, 'but would you mind awfully if Mrs Potter and I were to say grace?'

'Not at all, Reverend,' said the Professor. 'Even though we believe religion to be a pursuit of the feeble-minded, Smee and I are *cultural Christians* through and through, aren't we Smee?'

'Very much so.' A few days earlier the Professor had informed Smee of this. He had been a little taken aback, but had quickly adjusted to the idea. 'The Professor takes his cultural Christianity very seriously indeed, as do I.'

'Absolutely,' said the Professor. 'Just because religion is a heinous trick played on the credulous, century in and century out, there is no reason why I should go without my Christmas presents or Easter eggs. Tell them how many Easter eggs I ate this year, Smee.'

'Forty.'

'That's right – forty in one sitting, and I even ate the sweets in the middle. There was chocolate all round my mouth. I paid the price the next day though. Do you have any idea – any idea at all – what eating forty Easter eggs does to the human stool? It is really quite alarming.'

'I wasn't there at the time,' said Smee, 'but the Professor has shown me a series of Polaroids of the incident, so I have seen just how violently the body reacts to such a diet. It was, to put it mildly, horrifying.'

'It was worth it though. I do not regret a single egg, such is my commitment to cultural Christianity.' The Professor drifted into a reverie. 'Wispa ... Galaxy ... a Spider-Man one ... The foil made a ball the size of a tangerine ... Forgive me,' he said, snapping out of it. 'Please do proceed with your charmingly archaic incantation. Smee and I shall remain silent throughout as a mark of sensitivity.'

The Reverend closed his eyes, bowed his head and began. 'For what ...'

A partially stifled snigger came from one of their guests. The Reverend did his best to ignore it. He started again.

'For what we are about ...'

There was more sniggering, this time from both guests. The Reverend paused for a moment, reflected, and tried for a third time.

'For what we are about to receive, may the Lord make us truly thankful. Amen.'

Mrs Potter joined in. 'Amen.'

'Wonderful!' cried the Professor. 'That was like a window into the past. Who needs a time machine with you two around? You do realise, don't you, that you might as well have been speaking to a goblin with a purple face? There is no God, you know, just as there is no goblin.'

'I think for now we had better agree to disagree on that one, Professor. Gentlemen, bon appétit.'

The visitors had missed their usual teatime snack, and they tucked in enthusiastically. 'Convention dictates that I now pay my hosts a compliment,' said the Professor, 'and may I say that this cottage pie is delicious. One hesitates to use the word "divine" because of its supernatural connotations, but it is certainly extremely tasty.'

'Thank you, Professor,' said Mrs Potter. 'I'm so pleased you like it.'

'Yes, in spite of your shortcomings, you religious types are capable of producing decent foodstuffs,' said the Professor. 'I will give you that. Your Islamic rivals make a splendid baba ghanoush, not to mention hummus.'

'We had a lovely hummus on our trip to Jerusalem, didn't we dear?' said Mrs Potter. 'In that nice Jewish restaurant, do you remember? I think it was the best I've ever tasted.'

'Listen to yourselves,' snapped the Professor. 'That is just typical of you lot, incessantly pitting one religion against another. No wonder there are so many wars. The sooner you all realise you are wrong about everything the better. Your silly books are just collections of fairy stories; you might as well revolve your lives around the teachings of the Three Billy Goats Gruff. Science is the only way – and I am unanimous in that.'

'Ah, wonderful,' said the Reverend. 'I was hoping you would raise the topic of science. I happen to know that you have done a great deal of groundbreaking work in the field, Professor.'

'Yes, yes, I have done a number of experiments over the years, many of them rather fascinating.'

'The Professor is being typically modest,' said Smee. 'In fact he has done *all* the experiments.'

'I cannot deny it; although my primary field is biology, I have also done all the physics and chemistry ones. There is just no stopping me when it comes to science.'

'I'm afraid I must confess, Professor,' said Mrs Potter, 'that I have never had a great interest in science.'

'Then you can fuck off,' said the Professor.

Gently, the Reverend came to his wife's defence. 'Professor, wouldn't you say that was just a little on the rude side?'

Smee was surprised to find himself agreeing with a vicar; the Professor's outburst had not seemed particularly appropriate.

'Not at all.' The Professor was indignant. 'Science is all around us. It is everything, and if you are so blinkered, and so dull-witted that you cannot even muster a keen interest in it, then quite frankly you should never have been born. One of the other sperms should have got through, instead of the one that made you. And besides, I was quoting somebody and it doesn't count as rude if you're quoting.'

Smee was relieved to find himself convinced by the Professor's retort, and felt guilty for his moment of doubt.

Reverend Potter, though, pursued the matter. 'Perhaps so, Professor, but I do think it was a little over the top for the dinner table, and I wonder if you might say sorry to my wife.'

Smee watched the Professor, wondering how he was going to respond, but knowing he would do the right thing.

The Professor crossed his arms and made a Winston Churchill face.

'Come along, old chap,' said the Reverend. 'I'm not going to ask you to look as though you mean it. All I'm asking is that you say the words.'

'Very well,' sighed the Professor, 'if it means that much to you: I acknowledge that a swear word was quoted at the dinner table, and I request that we now draw a line under the incident and continue with our meal.'

'Consider it water under the bridge,' smiled Mrs Potter, who had faced a lot worse in her time, and forgiven far more extreme transgressions. Smee was amazed to see her carry on as if she hadn't just been told to fuck off. 'Now, speaking of water, there is one little question I hope you don't mind me asking,' she said. 'I'm afraid you'll find it rather elementary, but as I said I am not really of a scientific bent.'

'Ask away, but I should warn you that my answer will shake your faith to its very foundations.'

'It's a risk I am prepared to take, Professor. Now, I know that water turns to gas at a hundred degrees centipede.'

'Yes, yes, carry on,' said the Professor wearily, knowing exactly what was coming next.

'And evaporation happens when water turns to gas and goes up into the air. Am I right, Professor?'

'If you say so, Mrs Potter,' he yawned. 'Do continue.'

'So, I was wondering, if that is indeed the case then how come puddles aren't particularly hot? They evaporate, but they never seem to be all boiling and bubbling, do they?'

On his first day with the Professor, Smee had heard this question posed several times, and on each subsequent day it had reared up again, and every time it had come from somebody who seemed to think that, because puddles managed to disappear without ever becoming boiling hot, the whole of science must be wrong, or at best unreliable. The Professor rose to his feet and cleared his throat, and as he responded to Mrs Potter's question, Smee knew the words so well that he could almost have joined in. He spoke of diffusion, kinetic energy and vaporisation, and quite a lot about molecules, and though Mrs Potter was not able to follow it all, she was clearly doing her best to keep up.

'Fascinating,' she said.

'It is basic science, you know. You must understand, Mrs Potter, that there is much in the natural world which is not visible to the naked eye. I learned this during my undergraduate years at Cambridge University, or Oxford, whichever one it was – I am certain it would have been one or the other, but such trifling details tend to vanish amid the fog of achievement.'

'It was Oxford, Professor,' put in Smee.

'Ah, yes, Oxford. Of course, the dreaming spires and so forth. Not that I ever paid them much heed, so absorbed was I by what I observed as I crouched day and night over my trusty microscope. I found world after world, tiny galaxies that lay a long way beyond the sphere of normal vision. Droplets that you might see with those blue eyes of yours, Mrs Potter, are as skyscrapers to grains of sand when compared to the molecules involved in the process of evaporation. Even now, every time I look into a microscope, the first thing to cross my mind is how the people who wrote that absurd book to which you so desperately cling had no idea of any of this. They had no microscopes, no telescopes; their understanding of the world around them was but an infinitesimal fraction of what we now know. Imagine how much metal there is in a paper clip, Mrs Potter. Now imagine how much there is in the Eiffel Tower. That comparison does not even begin to convey the difference I am talking about. To use that book as your primary source of scientific knowledge is … Now how shall I put this politely? It is pathetic. So you see,' concluded the Professor, sitting down at last, 'it isn't fairy dust carrying the water away; there is a perfectly simple scientific explanation. As with all these things, it is not a miracle at all. Oh, and you know the clouds up in the sky? Those fluffy-looking things I mentioned in my explanation?'

'Yes, Professor.'

'I'm sorry to be the one to break the news, but they don't have angels on them, playing harps.'

The Professor and Smee laughed, and the vicar and his wife joined in a little too.

'Now, for the sake of form, I shall tell a single anecdote, following which I shall finish my meal in silence,' said the Professor. Wearily, he told the one about the time Stephen Jay Gould's trousers had fallen down on stage at a conference in Copenhagen. Then, true to his word, he drifted into a furious quiet.

It was left to Smee to make general conversation about the weather and the town. He relaxed into this role very well, even attaining something of a rapport with his hosts. He had to keep reminding himself that they had devoted their lives to peddling lies more dangerous than smallpox.

7

Back in the bedroom, Smee called Mrs Smith, his contact at the All Bottoms Women's Institute. He had spoken to her a few days earlier, when arranging the booking.

'Hello Smee,' she said. 'How lovely to hear from you. I do apologise for this terrible weather. It's come a bit early this year and taken us all by surprise.'

'It is a little inconvenient, isn't it, Mrs Smith? But the Professor is determined to honour his booking. I wonder, would you happen to know anybody with a hot air balloon we could commandeer?'

'Hmmm … let me think. No, I'm afraid not.'

'Or perhaps an elephant? We were thinking we could go down the Hannibal route.'

'I'm afraid we're all out of elephants at the moment, but don't you boys worry, we can postpone. Now here's an idea: on Monday we're all getting together for a charity event, so perhaps the Professor could come along and give his little talk then? Would that be convenient?'

Smee checked his diary. It was empty until the Wednesday of the following week, when the Professor was booked to give a presentation at a nursery school science club under the heading 'Fun with Dissection'.

'Monday sounds ideal,' said Smee.

'The event is starting at two thirty in the afternoon, so if you could turn up around then that would be super. Hopefully the trains will be running again but if not, never mind. We'll quite understand if you can't make it, and hopefully we'll be able to arrange something for another time. It does sound like a very interesting talk.'

Smee bade Mrs Smith goodbye and relayed the news to the Professor.

'But it's only Thursday. Good grief, Smee, are we really going to be stuck in this scienceforsaken place until Monday?'

'I shall do what I can to arrange an engagement or two while we are here.'

'See that you do.'

Normally if they had a stretch of time between bookings the Professor would continue his travels and present his findings and opinions in an ad hoc manner; Smee had seen him stand on an upturned crate in a shopping centre and give a rousing speech on the subject of how fossils were considerably older than churchgoers would have others believe, and watched him as he stunned the top deck of a bus one rush hour by chairing a furious debate on the existence or otherwise of fairies at the bottom of the garden. Smee decided that at the earliest opportunity he would head out into the snow and find a suitable venue, and see to it that the people of Market Horten were exposed to the wisdom they so desperately needed to hear.

'Now take a letter for me, Smee. A proper paper one this time – none of that electronic nonsense. We are going to transcribe my encounter with Dave the taxi driver and send it to my dear friend Martin Amis. He is always looking to get closer to the common man. Did you know he once spent an entire week living with a humble postman and his family? He sat in the corner of their drawing room, or "lounge" as I believe they called it, and took notes as they watched ITV. This will be invaluable to him; I can just see him weaving my little chat with Dave into one of those novels of his.'

Smee recalled the encounter differently from the way the Professor recounted it; he hadn't picked up on the natural, class-spanning bonhomie between the two men, and he was also a little dismayed to find that he had been entirely written out of the scene, but he transcribed away nonetheless. He reminded himself he was merely a bystander; the episode belonged to the Professor and the taxi driver, not to him.

'PS,' the Professor concluded, 'Please forgive the appalling handwriting. I have engaged the services of an amanuensis, and quite frankly you can't get the staff. That will be all, Smee. I don't have his home address to hand, so just send it to his agent, my dear friend the Jackal, and he will receive it by and by.'

Smee, accepting that his handwriting wasn't everything it could have been, addressed and stamped the envelope, ready to send it in the morning.

The Professor stretched out on the bed, hands behind his head. 'Amis will find that invaluable,' he said. 'I will never forget the time I was with him in the green room of the Cheltenham Literature Festival. He pointed to a huddle of supposedly promising young novelists on the other side of the room. "Those scruffs, Dawkins," he said, "they write villages. You and I, we write metropolises." Or was it "metropoli"? I can't quite remember, but you get the gist. I saw one of the promising young novelists later that evening, vomiting into a municipal shrubbery.' The Professor shuddered at the recollection before going to the bathroom to brush his teeth and change into his pyjamas.

When he returned, the men hunched close to Smee's computer as they caught up with the episode of *Deal or No Deal* that they had missed. The Professor shouted advice at the contestants, applauding them when they appeared to do as they had been told, and berating them if they disobeyed him. 'They would never let me on this show, Smee,' he said. 'I would win every penny.'

When the programme was finally over, the Professor announced that it was time for bed. Smee had shared a room with him several times over the course of the three weeks they had been travelling together, so he knew what he had to look forward to. The Professor would grind his teeth, and make involuntary outbursts throughout the night. Smee knew he would be woken several times as the sleeping Professor loudly declared that, 'There is no God,' or bellowed, 'It's a Creationist lie.' He had thought about buying ear plugs, but had decided that everything that came from the Professor's mouth was worth listening to, even when he didn't realise he was saying it.

Friday, 29th November

8

'You boys stay as long as you need to,' said Mrs Potter, refilling their teacups. 'We shan't be driving you out into the cold.' The snow had more or less stopped, but it was still drifting and the town remained cut off. 'We'll find a way to keep you busy. There's the library, and we've got some lovely pubs and cafés, and this evening they'll be switching on the Christmas lights in the town square. We were supposed to be having that nice Mr Tumble come and do it for us – you know, the clown from children's television. I can't see him making it here through all this weather though. Still, they'll get them lit up somehow. The whole town turns out for it. Maybe you two could come and watch?'

'I hardly think that would be appropriate, Mrs Potter,' said the Professor, angrily spreading apricot jam on his toast.

'Mrs Potter,' said Smee, sensing a booking, 'I happen to know a celebrity who could very easily step into Mr Tumble's shoes. Somebody who has even been on the television.'

'Really, Smee?' asked Mrs Potter. 'And who might that be?'

Smee looked at his travelling companion, and gave a discreet nod in his direction.

To Smee's surprise, Mrs Potter managed to interpret this without making one of her mistakes. 'Professor, do you think that in the event of Mr Tumble not being able to make it, you would do us the honour …?'

'I suppose I could find it within myself to say a few words and flick the switch,' he said.

'Are you sure, Professor?'

'Of course I'm sure.'

'That would be wonderful,' said Mrs Potter. 'I'll call the committee right away, and tell them we have a backup plan.'

She darted out of the room to the telephone in the hall, and Smee enjoyed a moment of quiet satisfaction at having as good as secured a high profile booking even before they had finished breakfast.

'No newspapers, Smee?' asked the Professor.

One of Smee's jobs was to fetch the papers in the morning, but today he had come back empty-handed. He had posted the letter to Martin Amis though, so the journey had not been wholly wasted, even though it was unlikely that any mail would be leaving the town that day. 'I'm afraid the delivery didn't make it through the snow, Professor,' he said. 'All the newsagent had left was *TV Choice*, and you won't need that because you already know when *Deal or No Deal* comes on.'

'Then would you check that computer thing of yours?

I am impatient to see whether they have published my letter.'

'Certainly, Professor.' Smee opened his computer, and after a few clicks he found what he was looking for. He angled the screen for the Professor, who gave a 'Psscchhffff' and shook his head.

'Why must they always remove the exclamation marks, Smee? Sometimes I wonder why I bother giving them all this free material if they won't even respect the basics of punctuation. Censorship, I call it. Still, at least my core message remains.'

Smee didn't want the Professor to know that he had thought the exclamation marks to be a little frivolous, and had removed them before sending the letter. He said nothing as he scrolled down to reveal the comments underneath. The Professor perused every one, praising those who agreed with him and tutting at those who did not. When Smee scrolled back to the top of the page, the Professor's eye was caught by a thumbnail image of a cartoon.

'Make that drawing bigger for me, would you, Smee?'

With some apprehension, Smee clicked on it. His misgivings were not unfounded: the newspaper's cartoonist had homed in on the letter and made it his subject for the day. In the drawing the Professor was in a pulpit, from which he was delivering an impassioned sermon to, among others, a gagged Archbishop of Canterbury and a startled-looking goblin with a purple face. The subtext was as clear as it was familiar: the Professor's modus operandi was comparable to that of the religious zealot. Smee knew what was coming next.

The Professor was a man of many mottoes, one of which was 'Investigation, not litigation'. On his first day with him, Smee had been briefed about this. One of his key roles would be to stop him from distracting himself from his experiments and his fight with religion by becoming involved in protracted legal battles. 'I must rise above it, Smee,' he had said, 'for in the cold light of day I can see that to do otherwise would make me no less an enemy of free expression than Pippa Middleton.' The Professor had shown Smee a laminated press cutting about the former royal bridesmaid's apparently successful attempt to stifle her fellow writers by instructing her lawyers to suppress a light-hearted parody of her prose style. 'And she is not alone,' he had said, showing him another laminated clipping, this time about Scarlett Johansson's efforts to drive a French novelist out of print for writing a character who resembled her. 'Speaking man to man, Smee,' he had confided, pointing at the sumptuous photograph that accompanied the news report, 'were the opportunity to arise, biology would take over and I would be in there like a rat up a drainpipe – and you cannot tell me there is a red-blooded man who would not behave likewise. She extends my phenotype, if you catch my drift, but that does not give her the right to tell people what they can or cannot put in a book. The only time I have ever sued anybody,' he had said, 'was when a rather downmarket clothing establishment by the name of Topshop started selling T-shirts with my face on. One has to draw the line somewhere.'

And this morning, as drifting snow piled up against the window and the Professor stared at the cartoon, Smee could sense that the red mist was descending, and he knew he was on duty.

'Call my lawyers, Smee,' the Professor hissed. 'I will not be caricatured. I will not be mocked. I have not devoted half a century to developing a trusted global brand only to have it compromised in this way. I will not be likened to religious maniacs. I will not be lampooned. Everybody must take me seriously, and this is something that needs to be enshrined in the law of the land.'

Smee knew exactly what to do, and he went through the script that he and the Professor had prepared for these eventualities. All the trigger phrases were in place to calm him down: investigation not litigation; to sue would do more harm than good to Brand Dawkins; intelligent people fancy Scarlett Johansson less since she did that; it is an obvious parody and it will not impact negatively upon your reputation; there would be less time to do experiments if you got tangled up in court. Then came the trump card: the repetition of the word 'Pippa'. Using all his strength, Smee pinned the Professor's flailing arms to his side and said the word over and over again. The Professor, as he knew he must, joined in. Gradually he calmed down, and their voices softened.

Mrs Potter came back into the room to find the men locked in an embrace and repeatedly whispering 'Pippa'. 'You are a funny pair,' she said. 'I've spoken to the committee, and they say they would be delighted to have you, Professor.'

The men disentangled themselves. 'There, Smee,' said the Professor. 'I have risen above it. Now, if I am not mistaken I have a speech to prepare.'

9

The men listened closely to Smee's pocket radio. 'The Bottoms remain blocked for the foreseeable future,' said the announcer, 'as do all roads in and out of Market Horten.' That was all they needed to know.

'Tumble's loss is our gain,' said the Professor.

It was nearing the time for the big switch-on, and he had a final glance over the speech they had spent the day honing and rehearsing. Apart from a short break for lunch, and a longer one to watch *Deal or No Deal* on the tiny television in their room, they had worked on it non-stop.

The Professor knew he had to adjust to the circumstances, and a full lecture would not be appropriate. 'This is science, not show business,' he had told Smee, 'but nonetheless, one must know one's audience.' After some deliberation he had decided that the best way to precede the switching on of the Christmas lights would be with a five-minute distillation of his views on the subject of infanticide.

'It galls me, Smee,' he said, 'that just because I have declared that I have no strict moral objection to the killing of children up to the age of one *in certain circumstances*, I am automatically labelled the new King

Herod. It is a textbook media distortion. If the story is to be believed, Herod wanted *all* the babies dead; I just broadly support the idea that *some* of them should be allowed to undergo post-birth abortions. There is a world of difference, and this engagement is the perfect opportunity to answer my critics and offer a concise clarification of my position on the subject.'

'I'm sure your audience will be thrilled, Professor,' said Smee. 'What an unexpected treat it will be for them.'

The Professor picked up his phone. 'I had better check in with number three,' he said, dialling. 'Hello dear. Yes, we are still stuck in the snow. No, I didn't get to see Upper Bottom, but I hope to on Monday at half past two.' He looked at the phone. 'It's gone dead again. Damnable reception around here, Smee.'

The men piled on several layers of clothes, ready to head to the town square.

10

The Professor and Smee stood in the wings of the makeshift stage. In spite of the weather, the place was packed with highly insulated townspeople of all generations, waiting for the lights to come on and for the Christmas season to officially begin.

'It is always invigorating to meet a mayor, Smee,' said the Professor, indicating the man with whom they had just spent a convivial two minutes and who was now donning his ceremonial chains and flicking through a thin wad of index cards as he readied himself to open the night's festivities. 'There is much to be said for rubbing shoulders with those who hold high office, just so long as one does not get carried away and lose the common touch.'

Activity backstage was becoming hectic. It even reached the point where a woman in black walked past with a wireless headset on, almost as if they were on the set of a daytime television show. 'It looks as though I shall be taking to the stage any minute now. Check my appearance, Smee.'

Smee went through his standard list: flies, nostrils, parting. 'All clear, Professor,' he said.

'You know, Smee, I think this could be one of the defining speeches of my career.'

Smee felt a pulse of satisfaction at the thought that he had played his part in this landmark in the Professor's life.

The theme from *Knight Rider* blasted out from a big stack of speakers, and laser lights shot into the night sky. A cheer went up, the woman in black gave the mayor the all clear and he walked on stage, fists clenched, and arms above his head.

The music died away. 'People of Market Horten,' he cried into the microphone. 'Are you ready for Christmas?'

The reply was a resounding 'Yyyyyyeeeeeeessssss'.

'I can't hear you.' He cupped a hand to his ear. 'I said, *are you ready for Christmas?*'

An even louder 'Yyyyyeeeessssssss'.

'You can do better than that. Market Horten, … are … you … ready … for … CHRISTMAAAAAAAAS?'

This time the response was almost deafening. Market Horten was ready for Christmas.

'I'm sure one or two of you will have noticed that we've been having a little difficulty with the weather, and getting people in and out of town has been pretty much impossible for the last twenty-four hours. I'm sorry to say that Mr Tumble hasn't been able to make it.'

There was a loud groan, and some children began to cry.

'But don't be downhearted. Another leading celebrity has kindly agreed to step in at short notice and take his place.' There was a rumble of anticipation as people speculated as to who this celebrity could be. 'Here he is, to give a few words before switching on the Christmas lights ...' The mayor looked at the index card Smee had written out for him, and read out the Professor's approved introduction. '... The only person ever to have received both the Deschner Award *and* the Medal of the Presidency of the Italian Republic; and the author of many books, among them *River out of Eden* and *The Extended Phenotype*. Will you please give a warm Market Horten welcome to the thrice-married evolutionary biologist Professor Richard Dawkins.'

There was a polite smattering of applause, and a few mumbles of, 'It's so nice to see he's finally out of that wheelchair,' as the Professor strode, with great poise, to the lectern that awaited him centre stage.

'Good evening ladies and gentlemen,' he said. He had been practising his 'fireside chat' voice all day, and his tone was authoritative yet avuncular. 'I am delighted to have been granted the opportunity to stand before you on this cold winter's evening and share with you my views on the rather thorny subject – let's not pretend otherwise – of infanticide.'

The general feeling among the audience was that he seemed like a very nice man, but they weren't quite sure why he wanted to talk about that sort of thing. As he continued his speech, the Professor noticed a humming noise, and wondered whether something might be wrong with the public address system. He soldiered on nonetheless. 'I'm sure there are those among you who would hold your hands up right now and say, "Hang on, Professor, infanticide is wrong. It can never be OK to kill children." Let me assure you that I fully understand your misgivings, but I do ask you to hear me out on this one ...'

The humming had become a buzz and the Professor looked up into the sky, to where it seemed to be coming from, and he saw a bright light. By this point everybody was looking towards this light and, as it grew closer, they noticed something extraordinary.

The light was coming from a helicopter, and underneath the helicopter, waving as he dangled from a bungee cord, was Mr Tumble.

11

The helicopter hovered over the town square as Mr Tumble bounced up and down, pulling funny faces. Toddlers who, moments earlier, had been inconsolable were now small beacons of delight as they were held up high by their parents to get closer to their idol.

The Professor remained behind his lectern, waiting for the hubbub to die down so he could resume his speech. There were several minutes of waving and face-pulling before the helicopter flew off to land on the nearby recreation ground. The woman with the headset came up to him. 'Sorry about the interruption,' she said. 'The last we heard he wasn't coming, but it'll take him a while to get to the stage, so you're back on.'

The Professor leaned into the microphone and cleared his throat to bring quiet over the excited throng. They didn't seem to notice. 'Excuse me,' he said. 'Simmer down.' This time the general feeling was, *Oh, it's that nice man again. I'd completely forgotten about him. Let's let him finish his little talk about insecticide, or whatever it was.* At last a respectful hush fell over the revellers, and the Professor picked up where he had left off. He emphasised that he was ready to allow consideration for those who worried that infant euthanasia could go too far, and that he accepted it would be hard to define just where boundaries should be drawn.

'And of course,' he said, 'I am acutely aware of the sensitivity surrounding this issue, but just because a matter is complex, does that mean it will forever be off the table? No, we must rise to meet it. So let us all go from here tonight and continue this discussion with friends, with colleagues, with neighbours, with relatives, with strangers, and with those who hold high office. As I stand before you on this rather chilly evening I tell you that I would have no moral objection to a little bit – just a tiny little bit – of infanticide. And …' It was time for his trademark sign-off. '… I am unanimous in that.'

The audience, almost none of whom had been paying the slightest attention, clapped enthusiastically and cheered when they realised he had finished. As the applause died down, Mr Tumble bounded onstage. He made a few jokes, did a few tricks and at one point fell over and got his head stuck in a bucket. The Professor remained centre stage as the clown weaved around him, waiting behind his lectern for his cue to switch on the lights. At one point Mr Tumble incorporated him into his act, inviting him to smell the large flower in his lapel and, when the Professor obliged, spraying him in the face with a jet of water. It all went down very well.

Mr Tumble disappeared into the wings, and the mayor bounded on to the stage. 'Ladies and gentlemen,' he said. 'Let's hear it for Mr Tumble!' The crowd went wild. 'But there's a problem, isn't there?' continued the mayor. 'It's not Christmas yet, is it? And do you know why it isn't Christmas, boys and girls?'

The audience chanted: 'Lights! Lights! Lights! Lights!'

'That's right – it can't be Christmas without lights. Who wants Mr Tumble to come back and switch on the lights?'

As yet another joyful roar went up, the mayor felt an urgent tugging at his sleeve. He turned to see the Professor. The two men had a brief conversation away from the microphone, and the mayor went back to his duties as Master of Ceremonies. 'And joining Mr Tumble in switching on the lights will be …' He quickly flicked through his index cards to remind himself who, with nobody by his side to restrain him, had just threatened him and his town with financially crippling court action unless he was granted joint top billing at the switch-on. '… The thrice-married evolutionary biologist Professor Richard Dawkins.'

The woman with the headset ushered both men over to the switch, where their fingers jockeyed for position. The mayor began the countdown. 'Ten … nine … eight …'

The crowd was in fine voice. 'Seven … six … five … four … three … two … one … CHRISTMAAAAAAAS!'

Together the Professor and Mr Tumble pushed the switch, and the town square became a shimmering wonderland, lit up with flashing snowflakes, holly leaves and reindeer pulling sleighs. The woman in black ushered a brass band on to the stage, and they started playing 'Merry Christmas Everybody'. As Mr Tumble led the dancing, the Professor waved goodbye to the crowd and weaved his way through the trumpets and past the tubas into the wings.

'I want a word with you, Smee,' he hissed.

The fireside chat was over.

12

The Potters were still out, helping on the mulled wine stall, so after walking back in silence the men had the house to themselves, which was just as well because the Professor's voice was at full, window-rattling volume. 'What', he raged, 'was the meaning of that?'

'I'm sorry about the clown, Professor,' said a trembling Smee. 'As I understand it, he had given up hope of getting here, but a last-minute opportunity presented itself so he took it. It's just a shame that the timing of his arrival was so unfortunate.'

'I have no quarrel with the clown, Smee,' he bellowed. 'He was buoyant and broadly secular, which are the primary qualities I look for in a circus performer. But what I wish to know is this: how does he have access to a helicopter while I do not? He was entertaining, Smee, but unlike me he was not important. Are you telling me that a bouncing clown's travel plans are considered more urgent than those of the greatest philosopher-scientist of his age? And if so, what wretched days are these in which we live?'

'It looked like an army helicopter to me,' said Smee. 'Maybe Mr Tumble has contacts high up in the military.'

'That taxi driver of yours told us there was no helicopter in the locale.'

'That's right, Professor.'

'And you just took him at his word?'

Smee nodded.

'That was a fatal error of judgement. Your friend Dave was not a reliable source of information. Had I known he was the kind of man who gave out misleading information about helicopters I would never have written to Martin Amis about him.'

'Perhaps you could relay this development to Mr Amis, Professor. It might make Dave a more complex and engaging character for his readers.'

'Perhaps I shall. But for now, let me tell you this: my last Smee would not have taken a simple cabbie at his word.'

Smee felt his head swim. He'd had no idea that there had been Smees before him, and he was terrified at the thought that there might be Smees yet to come.

The Professor had not finished. 'No, my last Smee would have ignored him and gone out into the snow and found me a helicopter before anybody else had a chance to nab it from under my nose. I would have been flown to Upper Bottom this afternoon and I would have given my talk to the Women's Institute as scheduled, and by now I would have been out of this ridiculous situation. Imagine me – the winner of the 2001 Kistler Prize – being snowed-in in a small town, trapped like a caged beast. Listen very closely, Smee: you need to raise your game. If you do not get me to the stage on Monday at half past two I shall have no choice but to terminate our arrangement.'

Smee trembled.

'Just have a look at that Internet thing you are always on,' said the Professor. 'There are millions who agree with everything I say, and who would give their eye teeth to be in your position. And another thing: you are getting a little too cosy with these Potter people for my liking. The female one seems harmless enough, but you seem to be forgetting that the male one, the so-called "Reverend", is part of the wicked religious machine that is out to destroy science and send us all back to the Dark Ages. He is a key player, a cracker of the whip, a subjugator, a teller of malicious untruths, a perpetuator of the phooey they call "scripture". Those manners of yours are inappropriate. "Yes, vicar. No, vicar. Three bags full, vicar." Would you be polite to him on the Internet? Of course not – so why be polite to him in real life? Do not forget for a moment what he believes in. I look forward to seeing you challenge him. I shall be watching you, Smee. I shall be watching you very closely indeed.'

'I'm sorry, Professor. I was just trying to be cordial, in line with your motto: Cordiality always.'

'That always was one of my lesser mottoes, Smee. In this instance I have modified it to this: Cordiality to a point. And I feel you have passed that point with these people. I expect you to rise to the battle at every opportunity; unless, of course, you happen to agree with them, and believe all that piffle, in which case …'

'I don't agree with them, Professor,' said Smee, hurriedly. 'Quite the contrary. In fact I completely *dis*agree with them.'

'You had better be telling the truth, Smee.'

'I am. I mean, it's all gibberish, isn't it? Fairy stories.'

At last the Professor's voice returned to its normal volume. 'I shall give you one tiny scrap of credit today, Smee: you did well in securing that booking. You will have noticed that in spite of the interruption my talk went sensationally well. Did you hear the applause when I finished? The audience was ecstatic. If ever a crowd was won over it was that one, and how was it won over? By my trademark combination of world-class oratory and irrefutable reasoning. And let us not forget the rock solid scientific foundation that underpins my every utterance, which in turn is backed up by all my doctorates and awards and television appearances and so forth. I'm telling you, Smee, something started here tonight in Market Horten. Tomorrow those people will talk to their friends and relations, and from here my message will spread, and not too many years from now people will think nothing of a little light infanticide; it will be as mainstream as toast.'

'I have no doubt of that, Professor.'

'Oh, and just so you know, when we were turning on those Christmas lights I applied considerably more pressure to the switch than the clown. What you saw there was 80 per cent Dawkins and only 20 per cent Tumble.'

The Professor decided on an early night, and Smee thought it best to join him. Before long the Professor was grinding his teeth and making occasional proclamations, but for a long time Smee could not sleep. He was worried about what the Professor had said about sending him back to his old life; the one he had plucked him from. For three weeks his days had been a whirl of excitement, but now, for the first time since meeting the Professor, he could feel the familiar sensation of melancholy eating away at him. A memory of the loneliness from which he had escaped hit him like a punch to the solar plexus. It didn't help that the party was still going on in the town centre, and when the icy breeze was blowing in their direction it carried the sound of music and happy voices.

His thoughts kept returning to the woman in black. He supposed she was still there, darting about with her headset on as she kept things running smoothly. He had spoken to her in passing, and thought she seemed very nice. He wondered what she was called, and where she was from, and all sorts of things along those lines.

Saturday, 30th November

13

Smee opened his eyes to find a pyjama-clad Professor standing at the foot of his bed. He snapped alert, overwhelmed by a sense of privilege at the exclusive audience he was about to have with the great mind.

'You will have noticed, Smee, a pattern: I enter a town, dazzle the locals with my erudition, ruffle a few ecclesiastical feathers and before they know what has hit them I am gone, leaving nothing but rational thought in my wake. The problem we are confronted with here is twofold: firstly, I am unable to move on thanks to ongoing adverse meteorological conditions; and secondly, most people in town heard me speak last night. It would be poor showmanship to follow such a triumph with a lesser event, so I shall instead have a day indoors, doing some experiments. It will be up to you to make your way around, furthering my reputation. See that you talk to all and sundry and make sure they are mulling over my speech. Start discussions in shoe shops and sidle up to old ladies at the launderette. I want infanticide to be the only topic of conversation in Market Horten today, and if anybody disagrees with my stance on it, go for the jugular just as you would if you were on the Internet. If they challenge you, tell them with great force that I have done all the experiments, and they shall be in no position to question my thinking until they too have done them. Now up you get and off you go.'

Smee looked at his watch. It was a quarter to five in the morning. His body hadn't woken as quickly as his mind, and he creaked out of bed. He had a shower, and shaved; by five past five he was fully dressed and back in the bedroom.

The Professor was setting up some apparatus on a small table. 'Goodbye,' he said, without looking up.

Smee left the room and stood on the landing with no idea where to go. He parted the curtains and peered through leaded panes to see that it was still night-time outside. Nowhere would be open for a long time to come, but the Professor had given him a task and he was ready to rise to it. He wondered whether there would be an early dog walker to talk to about infanticide, but on a day this cold even that wasn't likely. He was jolted out of his dilemma by a knock at the front door. It seemed somebody had saved him a lot of trouble and come to him. He went downstairs to see who it was.

He unbolted the door and opened it. A little girl of around eight years old was standing there, wide-eyed with worry.

'Mister,' she said, 'my mum says the nice science man is staying here, and he's the only one who can help. Is he here? Can you get him?'

The commotion had roused the Potters, and they came downstairs into the hall. 'Hello Emily,' said Mrs Potter, recognising the girl. 'Whatever is the matter?'

'It's our cat, Mrs Potter. She's having kittens and it's not going very well. She just keeps screaming and there aren't any kittens coming out, and it's been going on all night. The vet's stuck in the snow and my mum said the nice science man would know all about bliogoly, which is how cats have kittens.'

'I'm sure he'll know exactly what to do,' said Mrs Potter. 'Don't you worry, Emily. Smee will fetch him right away.'

Smee went back up to the room, where the Professor was moving some iron filings around with a magnet. 'Fascinating,' he was saying to himself. 'Absolutely fascinating.'

'Excuse me, Professor,' said Smee.

He didn't look up. 'You should know better than to interrupt me while I am conducting my experiments, Smee. Now leave the room.'

Smee did as he was told. As he stood on the landing he could hear voices from the hall. The little girl was sobbing. 'I'm just so worried about puss,' she wailed. The little girl's plight had awoken something within him and he felt compelled to give the Professor one more try before facing her.

He gently knocked at the door. There was no answer. He steeled himself and turned the doorknob. The Professor was still hunched over his iron filings, consumed by the science unfolding before him.

'Get out,' he roared. 'I am close to a breakthrough.'

Smee left the room again. He was annoyed with himself for having let sentimentality get the better of him. Here was one of the sharpest scientific minds there had ever been, and he was interrupting him from an experiment that for all he knew would change the course of history, and all because of a little girl and some kittens. What if somebody had burst in on Archimedes just as he was about to make his big discovery? Smee shuddered at the thought of living in a world where it had not occurred to a single person that bathwater went up when you got in. He told himself he hadn't woken properly and wasn't thinking straight. Ashamed, he went downstairs to the hall.

Emily looked up at him with large, tearful eyes. 'Is he coming, mister?'

'I'm afraid the Professor is in the middle of a very important experiment and must not be disturbed.'

'My mum said he was our only hope,' she sobbed. 'First dad dying and now this. It doesn't seem fair, Mrs Potter.'

Mrs Potter embraced her. 'There, there, Emily,' she said, giving Smee a disappointed look.

Smee knew that look well; his mother had given it to him many times as he was growing up. For a moment it was as if she was back, and he was a boy again, and it crushed him now as it had crushed him then. He couldn't stand it. 'Give me one last try,' he said. He raced upstairs and without knocking he entered the room.

'Have you taken leave of your senses?' bellowed the Professor, finally looking up from the swirls of metal powder, his eyes burning with fury.

'Professor, I have come to you on a matter of urgency.'

'Urgency? What could be more urgent than conducting an experiment the results of which will put to shame anything that has come from that silly Large Hadron Collider contraption? All the physicists have had their heads turned by that gimmick, and I am on the verge of sneaking in and beating them at their own game.'

'I'm sorry, Professor, but I really must insist you hear me out. A nearby cat is having difficulty in childbirth and your expertise is required.'

'The beast needs a common veterinarian, not an evolutionary biologist.'

'The vet is stuck in the snow, Professor.'

'Then we shall let the cat die, Smee; it is the natural way. She shall soon be no more, with the kittens just as dead inside her. All shall perish. Now good day to you.' He returned to his research.

As Smee turned to go, he had an idea. It would require the telling of a lie, but he recalled the look Mrs Potter had given him, and he couldn't bear to be given it again without making a final effort. He needed to know that he had tried his best. 'Did you read that item in the newspaper a while ago, Professor? The one about the Archbishop of Canterbury jumping into a lake and saving a dog from drowning?'

'Justin Welby can swim? I am amazed; he looks too weak to stay afloat.'

'By all accounts the Archbishop is rather good at the butterfly. The dog was having difficulties in a lake and in he went, cassock and all, and butterflied over to pull it out. And do you know what people said? They said that he had God on his side, and that if he hadn't been a committed Christian he never would have had the kindness to save the dog.'

'Kindness? Pah. I've told you a thousand times, Smee, only a Humanist such as myself can ever show true kindness. Humanism is by far the kindest of all the religions. Not that it *is* a religion, you understand; quite the contrary as a matter of fact. But I am a Humanist, Smee, not an Animalist. If Welby had even the slightest sense he would have known the hound was no more than a furry sack of chemicals and allowed it to drown. Fortunately I am no Welby, and I do not give a tuppenny damn about this moggie with which you seem to be so preoccupied. Cats are dying in misery every second of every day and there is no reason for this one to receive preferential treatment.'

'But Professor,' said Smee, at once ashamed and delighted by his own cunning, 'what if somebody from the local newspaper was to find out? If news were to get out that you had raced through the snow to deliver some kittens it could really show the Archbishop and his supporters that kindness does not depend on faith.'

'Her Majesty's Press, eh?' The Professor scratched his chin. 'I suppose that does put a different complexion on the situation.'

'Were your kindness to be observed and reported, your attendance at the scene would not be without its rewards. It would add considerable weight to your already gilded reputation, and further your cause no end.'

'Very well, Smee,' he sighed. 'Where is this creature?'

'In a nearby house, I would imagine. A small child will show us the way.'

'Then as soon as I have had my morning bath, changed into my day clothes and had a full English breakfast I shall be with you. I would also quite like to do a wordsearch before I go, and perhaps read an article or two from one of those *National Geographic* magazines that they have downstairs. And then it will be time for a snack. So maybe around eleven thirty? First things first, would you draw my bath for me, Smee?'

'Professor, please, if we wait much longer we might be too late.'

'So you expect me to throw on some clothes and race over to this cat's basket, do you?'

'That would make a marginally more positive story for the newspaper, Professor, than if you were to turn up hours from now to find a gravid corpse. As your male secretary, I implore you to make haste. The headline we are hoping for would be something along the lines of GODLESS BUT CARING ACADEMIC BRAVES SNOW TO DELIVER KITTENS; but you know what the media can be like, Professor, and we had better avoid giving them the opportunity to run the story under the headline ATHEIST VISITS DEAD CAT.' Smee had never been this assertive with the Professor, and he was surprised to find him responding positively.

'Oh, very well. I shall see you in the hall two minutes hence. But Smee, just remember that you are skating on thin ice. If this episode does not turn out to be a worthwhile use of my time ...' The Professor put a finger to his throat and drew it across while making a ghastly guttural sound. 'Not literally, of course, but I am sure you catch my drift.'

Smee hurried downstairs to deliver the news. He stood in anxious silence with the Potters and Emily, waiting for the Professor to arrive. He buried any thought that he might have been motivated by an innate desire to help the little girl; he knew from the Professor's writings that he had been born selfish and any altruism within him had been acquired. And neither, he told himself, did he care about anything as trivial as the wellbeing of a cat he had never even met. Instead he pushed to the fore the idea that all along he had been working towards arranging some positive press coverage for the Professor and his incredible ideas. He was desperate to get back into his good books and if his plan worked it would go a long way towards restoring and securing his position. He needed the Professor to consider him indispensible. He thought again of the life he had been plucked from just three weeks earlier, and he had no desire to go back there.

True to his word, after two minutes the Professor appeared, fully dressed. He oozed concern. 'I came as quickly as I could.'

14

There had been no fresh snow and the pavements had been trodden down to hard ice. The Professor and Smee took great care not to fall as they followed Emily.

'This takes me back, Smee, to when my own child was born. I think it was in the 1980s. I shall never forget the first time I held it in my hands. It was wriggling and crying and so on. I don't think I have ever felt anything quite like it; I was overcome by the most profound sense of cold scientific detachment.'

They turned a corner and entered a street packed with small terraced houses. The Professor tutted. 'I might have known we would end up somewhere like this.'

'We're here,' said Emily, opening the door to one of the houses. They stepped straight from the pavement into the sitting room.

'Fascinating, Smee. They don't even have a vestibule. To think people live this way.'

Smee chose not to mention that he had grown up in a house very much like this. It had just been him, his mum and his dad, and they had always made sure he was warm and clean and had food in his belly. It had been a home filled with love, and it saddened him that his memories of it were obscured by the frustration he felt at his own failure in adult life to live in a home filled with love.

Emily's front room was warmed by a wood-burning stove. The cat – black, white and furry – was still alive, and in a state of extreme distress. Emily's mother was trying, without any palpable success, to comfort it. 'Thank you for coming,' she said, a glimmer of hope in her tired eyes.

'Towels!' cried the Professor. 'Warm water and towels.'

Emily's mother hurried off and began to fill a washing-up bowl with water from the hot tap, while Emily ran up to the bathroom to get some towels.

'What kind of God would let a creature suffer so?' asked the Professor, looking at the distressed cat as it howled. 'A terrible God,' he said, in answer to his own rhetorical question.

Emily and her mother came back into the room, bearing the requested items. 'Now leave Smee and I with the cat.'

The mother and daughter withdrew. The Professor looked at the writhing animal, then at Smee. 'Of course you realise that if it comes to it I shall euthanise the beast.'

'Of course, Professor. But before you do so it might be judicious to inform its owners.'

'There will be no need for that. They would only protest in the simplest terms, and I have no patience for sentimental notions which prolong suffering. I shall take the correct course, unhindered by entreaties.'

'But first you will try everything you can to help it?'

'Yes, yes. But when the time comes, I wonder what the kindest way will be …' He looked around. 'So few households have their own surgical guillotine,' he sighed, 'but I shall make do with whatever is available.' He noticed a large antique mangle that was standing beside the hearth. 'Hmmm … Perhaps that would do the trick. I could feed the creature in tail first. Now you leave me too, Smee. Nobody is to enter until I say so; I shall face this alone.'

'Yes, Professor.'

Smee joined Emily and her mother at the table in the small kitchen. They sat in silence as appalling wails came from the room next door. Smee hoped that the Professor would not rush to kill the cat, that he would exhaust all avenues before resorting to euthanasia. He needed something to take his mind from the situation, and on the pretence of visiting the bathroom he took the opportunity to call the news desk of the local paper. He knew that if there was to be no media presence, questions would be asked and the thread his position was hanging from would be even more frayed than it already was. Even though a happy outcome was now extremely unlikely, he hoped the Professor's race to the scene would be kindness enough for a positive story. Nobody answered, so he left a message. The call over, he rejoined the mother and daughter at the table. The cat's condition did not seem to be improving.

The little girl turned to Smee and looked at him with enormous eyes. 'Mister,' she said, 'do cats go to heaven? If she dies will dad be able to stroke her?'

Smee heard the Professor's voice in his mind: *Tell her, Smee. Tell her she must not be so ridiculous. There is no heaven, not for her cat and neither for her father. You must cleanse her of the foolish notion that death is not the end. Perhaps you are willing to play your part in the outrageous manipulation of a young mind; but, if not, you must tell her the truth, that there is nothing out there but blind, pitiless indifference.*

'Yes, Emily,' said Smee. 'I'm sure cats go to heaven.'

After a few minutes the wails, which had become ever more excruciating, stopped. They exchanged glances, none of them daring to speak. Smee knew in his heart that the Professor would have deemed the cat to be beyond help, and with his trademark compassion allowed her a dignified exit. He hoped he had thought to drown her in the washing-up bowl, or smother her with the towels. The Professor killing an eight-year-old's cat by feeding it, tail first, through a mangle would be a hard story to spin positively to the media. He was having serious misgivings about whether he had done the right thing in inviting a reporter to the scene; the Professor posing for a picture alongside a lifeless furry pancake might not advance his reputation in quite the direction they had hoped. He supposed his mind still hadn't woken properly.

Emily and her mother were wide-eyed in anticipation, and knowing what they were about to find out, Smee couldn't bear to look at them. It seemed like an eternity before the door opened and the Professor came into the room. He was looking pale and even more serious than usual. 'It is over,' he said. 'You had better come through.'

Emily, her mother and Smee stood up and walked through to the sitting room, and there was the cat, in her basket, lying still on her side. She looked peaceful, exhausted but content, as four tiny mole-like kittens suckled at her teats.

Emily and her mother rushed up to the Professor and hugged him, tears of joy running down their cheeks. A little dazed, he accepted their embraces.

15

As they watched over the kittens and Emily tried out names for them, there was a knock at the door. In his relief, Smee had forgotten about the local newspaper, and it seemed the Professor had too; he hadn't once asked what had become of his promised encounter with the media.

Emily's mother opened the door to find a formidable aunt-like woman standing there.

'I have reason to believe a cat is having kittens on these premises,' she said, flashing her press card. She was invited in.

The Professor had regained a good deal of his composure. 'Ah, Her Majesty's Press,' he said. 'Always a delight. However, on this occasion I shall discreetly withdraw from the front line of newsgathering.'

'Are you the famous one?' she asked.

'That is not for me to say.' The Professor looked at Smee, who knew that it was for *him* to say.

'The Professor is rather well known. Indeed, he is widely regarded as the natural successor to Newton and Darwin,' he said.

'That's nice. I see the kittens are out, so congratulations are in order. Now let's get a picture.'

'You may take a photograph if you must,' said the Professor, 'but I am adamant that I shall not be available for interview.'

'Fair enough.' The reporter didn't seem to be in any way dismayed, and she directed the Professor, Emily and her mother to huddle around the suckling cats and smile for the camera. When the photograph had been taken the men went through to the kitchen to wash their hands and get into their coats.

'Are you sure you don't wish to speak to the reporter, Professor?' asked Smee.

'Had you been in the public eye as long as I, you would instinctively recognise an appropriate moment to get one's point across; this is not one of those times. When my dear friend Christopher Hitchens died, it was brilliant; I found myself with the perfect opportunity to reiterate to a hungry media, time and time again, my thoughts on the non-existence of God. I was able to hold him up as pure scientific proof that one does not cry out for salvation with one's dying breath. But, Smee, there are also instances when it best befits me to discreetly withdraw, and this is one of them.'

Smee hid his dismay. 'Very well, Professor. I hope you don't mind me asking, but … how did you get them out?'

'If you must know, I got the first one out with my fingers and the rest followed in quick succession.' Smee noticed that the Professor's hands carried scratch marks from the cat's claws. 'It was basic biology, but I shan't be telling that newspaper woman about it. I know what the press can be like. Can you imagine the headline? Archbishop of Atheists Puts Fingers up Cat's Whatnot.'

When they returned to the sitting room, the interview was in full swing: 'The Professor stopped his experiment and rushed over as quickly as he could … I don't know what we would have done without him … an expert biologist … such a kind man.'

Emily called the Professor over. 'See this one?' she said, holding in the palm of her hand a tiny kitten, jet-black save for white paws. The Professor took a long, close look at it. 'Mum's going to let me keep it and we're going to call it Professor, after you. We'll never forget you.'

'And I shall never forget you,' he said.

Smee could have sworn he saw a tear welling in the Professor's eye. *What a showman*, he thought.

The men said their goodbyes and left the house.

Smee knew that the Professor had been right to withdraw. The story would tell itself.

16

Mrs Potter was so delighted with the news of the safe arrival of Emily's kittens that she had insisted the men join them for an extra-large celebratory breakfast. Both of them were ravenous and accepted the invitation.

In spite of his hosts' best efforts to open up the conversation at the table, the Professor had managed to steer it time and again towards the subjects of science and religion. In her most recent attempt at general chit-chat, Mrs Potter had mentioned that she hoped their neighbours' chickens hadn't disturbed them with their clucking; the Professor had taken this as a cue to scoff at her for believing that chickens had been invented on the same day as snails, zebras, woodlice and all the other animals. Scoffing quickly escalated into fury. He turned red and repeatedly stabbed the table with his index finger as he told her that to deny the Theory of Evolution was tantamount to proclaiming that the Earth does not go around the sun.

'But I don't deny evolution, Professor. I'm no expert, far from it, but from what little I know, a lot of it sounds perfectly plausible – animals adapting to their environment and so on.'

'What nonsense. Of course you deny it. You are a

Christian, and you believe every word in that silly book of yours. If it told you there was a goblin with a purple face, you would believe that too.'

'Yes, Professor, I am a Christian, but I also happen to think that the Creation story in the Bible is a folk tale told to illustrate that God made everything. I do believe he did, but to take the account literally is a little on the simplistic side.'

'Let me tell you another name for folk tales, Mrs Potter: "Fairy stories". So there – you've said it yourself.'

Brilliant, thought Smee, in awe of the deftness with which the Professor cornered his quarry.

He carried on. 'I never cease to be amused by the way in which you religious people pick and choose. You love to quote the bits of scripture that suit you, while you disregard the parts that do not. Everything in your Bible is contradicted by something else in your Bible. Ask yourself this: what kind of God would leave such a mishmash for people to live by? I shall tell you what kind of God: a sly God, a nasty God. It is just as well for all of us that He does not exist. Unfortunately for Smee and I, it is simply not possible to pick and choose our favourite bits of science, because we believe in real things that are backed up by evidence, not silly made-up stories. Evidence, that is our watchword: evidence, evidence, evidence. Where is the evidence for your God?'

'I see it everywhere, Professor. Even in you, believe it or not.'

'Pah. I am talking about scientific evidence, not vague hunches.'

'I do think, though,' said Mrs Potter, 'that it is possible to be religious and still interested in science.'

'What rot.'

'There's a man who comes to our church who has his own Bunsen burner,' she said.

'And tripod and gauze,' put in the Reverend. 'He showed me round his laboratory. Well, it's his shed, really. Do you have a shed, Professor?'

The Professor chose not to talk about sheds. 'You either believe in science or you believe in religion; you cannot have it both ways. Tell her, Smee.'

Smee realised that the Professor was testing him, to see whether or not he was willing and able to stand up to the Potters. 'The Professor is right, Mrs Potter,' he said. 'To believe in religion is to believe in miracles, and miracles are by their very nature unscientific. Religion is an insult to science and an affront to reason.'

'I couldn't have put it better myself,' said the Professor.

Smee felt a warm glow at the Professor's approval, and thought it best not to compromise the moment by mentioning that he was directly quoting him.

'We had better agree to disagree on that,' said Mrs Potter.

'There you go again,' sighed the Professor. 'It's always "Let's agree to disagree," or "That would be an ecumenical matter." You people always try and wriggle out of healthy debate. You think you can trump us with a cliché here, a facile comment there, but let me tell you this: I am *not* agreeing to disagree.'

'Tell me though, Professor,' said Mrs Potter, choosing not to rise to the fevered level of debate asked of her by her house guest. 'There's something I don't quite understand about the Theory of Evolution, and I wonder if you would help me out.'

'There's plenty you don't understand about it.'

'Of course there is. As you know, I'm happy to admit that I've always found science to be beyond me, but I do watch nature programmes from time to time so I'm not completely useless. Now, Professor, I was wondering, if Charles Dickens's theory is correct, then one kind of animal changes into a completely different kind of animal. Am I right?'

'In a manner of speaking,' he sighed.

'Then why now, at this moment in history, are animals not changing into other animals? Why are we not seeing sort of in-between creatures being born? Why have monkeys given up on trying to be humans? And where are all the hairy fish, flapping about by the water's edge? And while we're on the subject, my husband has always wondered why men still have nipples after all these years. How come they haven't evolved away?'

The Reverend nodded an acknowledgement of the veracity of his wife's statement.

'Hairy fish and men's nipples?' sighed the Professor.

'If only I were able to say that I have never heard such nonsense in all my life.'

Smee understood the Professor's exasperation. Everywhere he went, he met people who asked him to explain the absence of hairy fish and the presence of men's nipples, using each as a reason for their scepticism about Darwin's theory.

'Let me explain,' said the Professor, rising to his feet. 'Though I warn you, it will be a little more than your weak minds can cope with. In a nutshell …'

Smee looked on in wonder as the Professor launched into an extraordinary spiel. Even though he had heard it all many times before, he was still barely able to comprehend a word of it. This was deep science, special knowledge that was accessible only to those with intellects incredible enough to process it. He was ready to acknowledge that his intellect was not up to the task, but he had absolute belief that the Professor knew precisely what he was talking about, that he dealt only in hard scientific facts, and that the conclusions he came to were, without exception, monuments of truth.

'And that,' concluded the Professor, ten minutes after he had begun, 'is why there are no hairy fish and why men have nipples.'

'Well, that is certainly one way of looking at things, Professor,' said Mrs Potter.

'One way? It is the only way. These are not opinions, Mrs Potter, they are facts, and they must be accepted as such. I have thirteen doctorates, you know. Which one of those do you believe disqualifies me from speaking with authority on my area of expertise?' He sat down. 'Now will you please let me get back to my breakfast? Look, my Golden Nuggets have gone all soggy.'

17

Reverend Potter had been given a strict talking to by his wife at bedtime the night before. 'No matter how confrontational he becomes,' she had said, 'you mustn't feel you have to leap to my defence. As you know, I've faced much worse over the years, and I can look after myself. And besides, I can't help feeling a little sorry for him. He must have had rather a rotten life to be so cross all the time.'

So as the Professor, his cereal bowl empty at last, banged the table and roared, 'Tell me Mrs Potter, are you ignorant, stupid, insane or wicked? Well? Which is it?' the Reverend merely buttered another slice of toast.

'Are those the only choices I have?' replied Mrs Potter.

'I'm afraid so.'

'Just insults?'

'But you will insist on disagreeing with me, Mrs Potter, and I have unanimously decided that anybody who disagrees with me must be at least one of those things. Even *you* admit that your book is a collection of fairy stories, yet still you cling to it. I would say that places you firmly in the *stupid* camp.'

Smee never ceased to be impressed by the efficiency of argument that arose whenever the Professor was involved, and he smiled at this latest checkmate.

'That's not very kind of you, Professor,' said Mrs Potter, looking a little sad. Smee felt a thud of confusion when he found himself feeling sorry for her and wondering whether she might have a point.

'I hope that you do not mistake my frankness for a lack of compassion. I am here to help you, Mrs Potter, to open those eyes of yours to the absurdity of your religion. When confronted with somebody like you, I feel I must take something of a "cruel to be kind" approach.'

Smee was relieved to hear this.

'I have no doubt that your heart is in the right place, Professor,' said Mrs Potter, 'but quite honestly I don't see how you think that anybody is going to suddenly start agreeing with you just because you call them names.'

'Mrs Potter, I am a great believer in the Golden Rule: Do as you would be done by. And I know for a fact that if I was unfortunate enough to be a Christian, I would be grateful for somebody with common sense to come along and be kind enough to speak to me plainly, and point out the error of my ways.'

'So you're being caring, Professor? That is very thoughtful of you.'

'I am an extremely caring person. I devote a lot of time to charity work, you know.'

'Oh, really? Which charities do you support?'

'Most of my energies are devoted towards one in particular: the Richard Dawkins Foundation for Science and Reason. I am a great believer in reason. I would even go so far as to say that I am one of the most reasonable people I know. Wouldn't you agree, Smee?'

'Absolutely, Professor.'

'See, it's not just me saying it; Smee thinks so too. And if you ask any alternative comedian, they will back him up. Very bright sparks, that lot, every one of them a huge supporter of mine. If you are looking for an expert to teach you all about how the gaps in the fossil record in no way challenge the Theory of Evolution, you could do worse than call on an alternative comedian. They have all read my books on the subject, and many of them have even memorised several of the relevant long words. There is little they could not tell you about the archaeopteryx, or xiangshuiosteus wui, or even orintagrathy. I cannot say I am a huge fan of their genre, however; to me it seems to be more of an alternative *to* comedy. But they would all agree, Mrs Potter, that my foundation is one of the finer charities. Do let Smee know should you wish to make a donation.'

The Reverend, exhausted and more than a little bored by it all, was relieved when a knock at the door gave him an excuse to leave the table. He went to answer it, and found one of his elderly neighbours standing there carrying a large and forlorn potted plant.

'Is the biology man here, vicar?' asked the neighbour. 'I'm hoping he'll be able to give me some advice about getting my poor yucca back to its old self.'

'We can but ask, Cyril. Do come in. Let me take that for you.' The Reverend held the plant as the visitor took off his coat and scarf and hung them up. 'A gentleman is here to see you, Professor,' he called through to the dining room.

'Send him in, if you must.'

The Reverend ushered Cyril through to the dining room, then drifted off to the kitchen for a respite from his visitor, absent-mindedly taking Cyril's plant with him.

'What can I do for you?' asked the Professor.

'My name is Cyril,' said the visitor, a bag of nerves in the company of so charismatic a character, 'and I have a bit of a problem. You see it's been a little droopy lately, and I was wondering if you could help.'

'Why should I assist in such a matter?'

'I hear you are an expert biologist; maybe you could tell me what the problem is. I've been giving it all my usual care and attention, but no matter what I do it just won't perk up.'

'Very well. Pull your trousers down.'

'Pull my trousers down?'

'Trousers down,' ordered the Professor.

Cyril stood frozen.

'Do you wish me to solve your problem or not? I am the eminent biologist around here, and I say take your trousers down. Come along, come along, my time is extremely valuable.'

At last Cyril did as he was told. He unclipped his

braces and his trousers fell to his ankles to reveal a pair of gigantic underpants.

'Is this really necessary, Professor?' asked Mrs Potter.

'Of course it is necessary.'

'Then I should leave the room.' She made to stand up.

'Not at all. You of all people would benefit from seeing some science in action.'

'What do *you* think, Cyril?' asked Mrs Potter.

He looked overwhelmed by it all. 'If the scientist says it's OK ...'

'Even so, Cyril, I ...'

'It's all right, Mrs P. He's the expert, so we'd better do as he says.'

Mrs Potter slumped back in her chair. 'Carry on, Professor.'

'I shall,' he said. 'And now lower those gigantic underpants of yours, Cyril. Come along now.'

Cyril lowered his gigantic underpants and stood in the Potters' dining room, his glory revealed.

'Well, well, well,' said the Professor, leaning forward to get a better view. 'I see. What a pity for you. I cannot imagine it regaining its vitality at any point in the future. Just be glad of your memories and find some new interests.'

'You don't think I should get another one?'

'Good grief, no. What a preposterous suggestion.'

'So ... are you saying I should just give up on it, Professor?' asked Cyril, despondent.

'Precisely.'

'But I've had it such a long time.'

'All good things come to an end.' The Professor pointed at Cyril's penis and said to Mrs Potter, 'I cannot imagine you requiring any further proof than this that there is no God.'

For the sake of Cyril's dignity, Mrs Potter had been doing her best to look away, but having heard so much about it she wasn't able to stop herself from glancing in its direction. Silently, she conceded that it didn't make for an encouraging sight.

Cyril pulled up his gigantic underpants and his trousers, thanked the Professor for his time and left the room just as the Reverend reappeared in the hall, holding the plant.

'I do apologise, Cyril,' said the vicar. 'I wandered off with Exhibit A. I suppose it would help if the Professor was to see it.'

'Well, no, as a matter of fact,' said Cyril. 'He was able to tell me all about it just by looking at my willy. It's incredible what scientists get up to these days; their methods have certainly changed since I was at school. Unfortunately, he says it's a hopeless case.'

The Reverend was able to piece together just enough of the story. 'Before you do anything rash, maybe you could try moving it to a different part of the house. I find that sometimes helps. And hang on a moment ...' The vicar disappeared before coming back with a bottle of plant food. 'There's a bit left in here; you finish it off. Give it a few drops and see how it goes. Just have a try before throwing it on the compost heap.'

'Right you are, Reverend. Thank you ever so much.'

Moments after Cyril left, the bell went again. This time it was one of the local boys, with his bicycle. 'Hello vicar,' he said. 'My brakes keep sticking, and my dad said there must be a scientific explanation so I should bring my bike round to the science man to see if he can help.' Determined to ensure that there were no further penis-based misunderstandings, the Reverend personally attended the boy's consultation, during which the Professor did indeed fix his brakes.

'Remember,' he said to the boy. 'They were fixed by basic scientific principles, not by prayer, and absolutely not by a goblin with a purple face.'

'Thank you, scientist,' said the boy, who was swiftly replaced by a woman who had recently dug a pond in her garden and wanted to know how her goldfish would cope in the cold weather.

18

Following the Professor's final consultation of the day, during which he had explained how food gets into tins, he and Smee went up to their room. The iron filings and magnet were where they had been left all those hours before.

'Perhaps you would like to return to your experiment, Professor?' said Smee. 'I can assure you I shall not interrupt this time.'

'The moment has passed. I was on the verge of inventing a vehicle propelled entirely by magnets, but I shall never be able to retrace my steps, so intricate were my calculations. I was within reach of a Nobel Prize, but no matter; it's a silly prize anyway. Quite honestly I wouldn't accept it even if they offered it to me. What is important is that the kittens arrived safely.'

Smee felt a pang of guilt for having inadvertently derailed a potential solution to the world's energy crisis. But, as the Professor himself had said, at least the kittens had arrived safely.

'That vicar is a hopeless case,' said the Professor, reclining on his bed, 'but I believe I am at last getting through to his wife. One cannot beat ridicule and mockery for making somebody come around to one's point of view. By the time we leave here she will have abandoned Christianity and converted to Humanism, you mark my words. Now pass me those leaflet things, Smee.' Mrs Potter had handed them a bundle of takeaway menus to go through; both men had built up quite a hunger, having only grazed on snacks in the moments between their many visitors.

The Professor leafed through them. There was one for the China Palace, and another for the Spicy Samosa, both of which seemed to gain his approval. 'It's all looking very tasty so far,' he said. The atmosphere changed when he got to the menu for the Kebab Experience. 'What is this?' he cried. 'I cannot allow it. It is an outrage.' Smee looked at the menu and realised at once the mistake the proprietor had made. 'Take a letter for me, Smee.'

Smee rushed to open his computer.

'It is to my dear friend the acknowledged punctuation expert Lynne Truss: Dear Lynne, I do hope you are well. I am in good health, thank you, though somewhat snowbound at present. I am sorry to report that I have just read a takeaway menu for a culinary establishment, upon the front page of which it is announced in letters almost one centimetre high that they provide – quotes – the best kebab's in Market Horten – close quotes. I am sure you will agree that this is an illiterate disgrace. From your dear friend Dickie Dawkins. Send that via one of those email things, would you?'

Smee sent the email. Minutes later a reply came in.

'Read it to me would you, Smee?' said the Professor, who was still trying to decide between the finalists: Luigi's Pizza and A Plaice For Us.

Smee glanced over it. 'I'm afraid I would rather you read it yourself, Professor. The language is somewhat ... creative.'

'No, Smee, you read it out.'

Smee braced himself and began. What followed was a beautifully punctuated stream of obscenities. Every comma, every semicolon was exactly where it was supposed to be as the Professor's correspondent railed in the most forthright terms imaginable against the kebab menu. 'Go in there and tell them where they can stick their "kebab's", Dickie,' she concluded, before adding, in case she hadn't made herself entirely clear, 'Up their "arsehole's"!!!!!!!'

'Wonderful,' cried the Professor, looking at the screen. 'Seven exclamation marks: exactly the correct amount. I see a lot of myself in that girl; if I hadn't thrown myself into the world of science, I would almost certainly have gone down the punctuation route. I'll never forget the afternoon I spent with her at a charming little book festival in Hay-on-Wye. We were strolling around the town after our respective lectures in the Barclays Wealth Arena when she spotted a misplaced hyphen on a greengrocer's blackboard and went absolutely berserk. She attacked the sign, and with just hands, feet and teeth she reduced it to a pile of splinters in less than twenty seconds. You should have seen the shopkeeper,

Smee; he curled up like a cashew and sobbed. Now, to business: Luigi wins. Give him a call.'

Forty-five minutes later the men were sitting on the ends of their beds with their pizzas on their laps, looking at Smee's computer as they re-watched a recent episode of *Deal or No Deal* with which the Professor had been particularly taken.

While the Professor whooped and groaned at the action on the screen, Smee found himself only half concentrating. There was a part of him that was wondering whether the woman in black from the night before was still in town, and whether she would be having a night out. He wished he was with her. He even started to think about going out and finding a nice pub, having a drink or two and looking out for her. But when the pizza was gone and the game show over, the Professor yawned and stretched. 'Bedtime for us, Smee,' he said.

'Yes, Professor.' He looked at his watch. It was only half past nine. He told himself it had been a long day and there would be much to do in the morning. He still had a mammoth task ahead: he had repeatedly assured the Professor that he would get him to Upper Bottom the day after tomorrow, and he still had no idea how he was going to do it. He reached for his wash-bag.

'One last thing, Smee.'

Smee reminded himself that he was ready to do anything for the man. 'Do you wish me to check you for haemorrhoids again?'

'No, everything appears to be tickety-boo in that department. Just go on that computer thing of yours for three or four hours and attack people who disagree with me, would you?'

'Nothing would give me greater pleasure, Professor,' said Smee.

'Always remember, Smee, that I have done the experiments that entitle me to my views. There is a healthy debate to be had, of course, just so long as everybody involved accepts without question that I have presented incontrovertible facts. Anything else is quite simply *un*healthy debate and must be stamped out at its first appearance. Anybody who agrees with me is of course free to use my facts as if they had done the experiments themselves. And those who do not agree … well, you know what to say to them, don't you, Smee?'

'I certainly do.' Smee got straight on to his task, but after just twenty-five minutes he found his mind wandering. He kept thinking about the kittens, and the woman with the headset. With the Professor asleep, he typed his final incandescent contribution to the comments section of an Internet news site, and closed his computer.

'There is no God,' declared the sleeping Professor. 'I am the expert, and I am telling you that there is no God.'

Smee switched off his bedside light and buried his head under his pillow, hoping for a good night's sleep.

Sunday, 1st December

19

'How lovely, Professor,' said Mrs Potter, looking at the front page of the *Sunday Express*. The main road into town had been ploughed and gritted and a newspaper delivery had made it through. The main headline was Snow Joke: Cold Snap Causes Travel Chaos, but in a box at the bottom of the front page was a photograph of their guest posing with the kittens under the heading Professor of Hearts. A short paragraph underneath took up the story: 'Snowbound evolutionary biologist Professor Richard Dawkins, 72, has been displaying his softer side by assisting the residents of a small town with all their science needs, including delivering a healthy litter of kittens and reassuring people about their goldfish. Full story p. 7.'

They huddled around the newspaper as Smee turned to page seven. Several of the Professor's visitors from the previous day had spoken to the reporter in Market Horten. Smee was relieved to see that she had either not found out about the Cyril incident, or had been too tactful to mention it. The Professor had not been disabused about the episode, but Smee had been told the story by a guiltily gleeful Reverend and Mrs Potter. To his shame, he had found himself joining in with their enjoyment of this latest mildly amusing misunderstanding.

The story of the Professor's impromptu advice clinic had been picked up by the *Express*'s London desk as well. 'The Professor was unavailable for comment,' the article concluded, 'though his British Humanist Association colleague A. C. Grayling, 64, appeared on the steps of the organisation's headquarters on Tottenham Court Road to sing his praises. "It doesn't surprise me at all that Richard has been caught red-handed doing good deeds," said the twice-married philosopher. "He is a Humanist, and we Humanists are all extremely nice people who do kind things with no ulterior motive. That is one of the many reasons why Humanism is the fastest growing religion in the world. Not that it is a religion, you understand; quite the contrary, as a matter of fact."'

'Good old Grayling,' said the Professor. 'He's not a bad chap at heart, and he does try very hard, but when it comes down to it mine shall always be the more convincing voice in the world of atheism. Let's face it, he has hardly done *any* of the experiments, and quite frankly the less said about his hair the better.'

Smee was quietly delighted by the coverage and hoped the Professor would recognise his contribution to this excellent press.

'You've done very well, Professor,' said Mrs Potter. 'I think you should celebrate with an egg. Boiled, poached or fried?'

'Poached, if you will.'

'And you, Smee?'

'Poached also, Mrs Potter. Thank you.'

Mrs Potter left the room, and after a long and awful silence the Professor turned his attention to the vicar. 'You have one thing going for you, Reverend,' he said.

'Oh, do I? How nice. What is it?'

'You are an *ex*-vicar. At least you're not still out there bleating on about Noah's Ark. As if the Creation story wasn't enough, you lot have to add insult to injury with that little corker.'

'I'm sorry to report, Professor, that I have *nothing* going for me. I still keep quite busy on the old vicaring circuit. I no longer have my parish, but I do quite a lot of filling in. It's not often a Sunday goes by without my donning the cassock for one reason or another. I shall be doing the honours at St Andrew's Church this morning at ten o'clock. You gents are both very welcome to come along.'

'I don't think so, Reverend. Cultural Christian though I am, it would hardly sit comfortably with my prominent involvement in the New Atheism movement to be seen turning up in church and listening to you babbling on about rumours of some rather unconvincing conjuring tricks from two thousand years ago.'

'Up to you, Professor. If you change your mind, you'll be most welcome.'

'Hmph. Hell will freeze over before you see me in your church. And that will be an awfully long time, since there is no such place as hell – hot, cold or otherwise. Isn't that right, Smee?'

'I'm afraid so, Reverend Potter. The Professor is absolutely correct.'

There was another long silence, soundtracked by the ticking of a carriage clock on the mantelpiece.

'Damn and blast it,' said the Professor. 'How long can it take to poach an egg?'

'An awfully long time, Professor,' said the vicar.

The silence resumed. Eventually Reverend Potter broke it. 'So tell me, Professor, you seem to be very interested in talking about science and religion, but do you have any other fields of interest? Hobbies, perhaps?'

'My interests and activities outside the opposing spheres of science and religion are best described as manifold.'

'Manifold?'

'Manifold.'

The vicar waited for the Professor to continue, but instead he furiously poured himself a top-up of tea and gave no indication of an intention to pursue the conversation.

'I wonder if you wouldn't mind telling us what you get up to when the old lab coat comes off?' asked the vicar. 'How does the great scientist unwind? What might one or two of these manifold interests be? Golf, perhaps? Sailing?'

'Brand management. I take an active interest in the

development, promotion and protection of the Dawkins marque.'

'I'm not entirely sure that counts as a hobby, Professor.'

'Then *Doctor Who*, if you must know,' he mumbled.

Smee backed him up on this. 'Oh yes,' he said, 'the Professor is very keen on *Doctor Who*. He has all the available episodes on DVD.' As Smee was an ardent fan of the show himself, they had often passed the time on long journeys by discussing its ins and outs over the decades.

'And I have the audio recordings of the lost episodes,' said the Professor, warming to the conversation. 'As well as a few under-the-counter curiosities, if you catch my drift.' He tapped his nose.

'The Professor is well known among aficionados for his impressive collection of memorabilia,' said Smee.

'I certainly am.' His eyes narrowed, and he even smiled a little. 'As a matter of fact, I have the *ultimate* in *Doctor Who* memorabilia.'

'A Dalek?'

'*Better* than a Dalek.'

'A Tardis?'

'*Better* than a Tardis.'

'Tom Baker's scarf?'

'*Better* than Tom Baker's scarf.'

'Even better than Tom Baker's scarf? I give up.'

'I shall leave you guessing,' he said, leaning back in his chair looking very, very pleased with himself.

Smee, who knew what the Professor was talking about, maintained a discreet silence.

'Very well. But how about other interests?'

The Professor gave Smee the look that told him he no longer wished to speak, and it was up to him to field the question. Smee picked up the baton straight away. 'The Professor is keen on …' His mind was blank. He couldn't recall the Professor ever having mentioned any further interests. 'Which is to say he is *extremely* keen on …' Smee knew he had to say something. Close to despair, he blurted out the only thing he could think of: '… *Deal or No Deal*.'

'Absolutely,' concurred the Professor, unable to stay silent when his joint-favourite programme was under discussion. 'What a show. If I ever meet that Edmonds man I shall shake his hand.'

'I've seen that once or twice,' said the vicar, 'but I can never quite work out what's going on.'

'It is not aimed at sub-par intellects such as yours, Reverend Potter.'

'I suppose not. Anything apart from watching television shows?'

The Professor looked at Smee, who was frantically trying to recall all the things he had read about the Professor. He had done his best to memorise his Wikipedia entry, but he couldn't recall there being a great deal about outside interests; it was all science, religion and tireless charity work. He panicked, frantically trying to recall any references to hobbies or other preoccupations. 'Opera,' he blurted.

'Ah, yes,' said the Professor, to Smee's great relief. *'Aida. La Traviata. La Bohème.* All the operas. If there's one thing I am passionate about, it is opera.' He put one arm to his belly and the other out to his side, took a deep breath and sang a very long and vaguely operatic note. When, at last, it finished, he took another deep breath and repeated the performance. When this encore finally came to an end he pointed a thumb at the Reverend. 'Tell him some of my other interests, Smee.'

Smee's mind seemed to him to be blank, but his lips moved anyway. 'Listening to other sorts of classical music.'

'Naturally. Beethoven, Mozart, Mahler, that one from the Hovis advert. Wonderful stuff. I have no patience for any of that music one hears in shopping centres and the like. Pip music, I believe they call it.'

'*Pop* music, Professor,' said Smee.

'*Plop* music would be more appropriate. Make a note of that quip, Smee, and be sure to recount it to anybody who has the audacity to say that I will not countenance levity. Continue, if you will.'

Smee's confidence was building now. 'Shakespearean plays.'

'Of course. You cannot beat a good Shakespearean play. "To be, or not to be", that kind of thing. "Once more unto the breach", and so forth.'

'"There are more things in heaven and earth, Horatio,

than are dreamt of in your philosophy,'" put in Reverend Potter.

'Pah. The trouble with Shakespeare is that he was writing in the olden days. If he was writing now there would be no mention of heaven in his works, except perhaps to say in no uncertain terms that it only exists in the fevered imaginations of the less able members of our species. The likes of you, for example. I think he and I would have got along rather well; he might even have helped us launch one of our atheist buses. He would have made a welcome change from the usual parade of alternative comedians. Well meaning as they are, one does tire somewhat of the same old faces: that Ince creature; the Minchin child. They all tend to become a little overexcited in my company. Did you see our latest bus in the newspapers, vicar? It was a splendid double-decker with "Keep Sunday Secular" written on the side in enormous letters. Like this.' The Professor lifted his pullover to reveal a T-shirt with the slogan on it. 'I always wear it under my smart clothes on a Sunday. Keep going, Smee. More of my hobbies, please.'

'Reading poetry.'

'Yes, the great poets. Keats, Yeats, Kipling, my dear friend Felix Dennis, Wordsworth … Next, Smee.'

Smee began to relax. He had already managed to build up quite a repertoire of interests for the Professor, and anything from this point on would be a bonus. 'Looking at art,' he said.

'I am forever looking at art. Proper paintings, you understand, none of that contemporary rubbish. *The Hay Wain*, *The Laughing Cavalier*, work of that ilk. Continue, Smee. A few more, to round things off.'

Smee felt he was on a roll now. 'Fine wine. Classic cars. Making jam. Horse-riding. Hillwalking.'

'Yes, yes, yes, no and yes. I cannot fathom where you got horse-riding from, Smee, but otherwise a faultless list. See, vicar, what did I tell you? My secondary interests are manifold. Now where on earth are those blasted eggs?'

20

The Professor fidgeted in the rear pew. 'Little wonder nobody goes to church any more,' he grumbled. 'The least they could do in this day and age is provide comfortable seating; but no, they cling like limpets to the old ways. No matter, Smee. The more uncomfortable the seats, the sooner this confounded organisation shall perish. Already it is withering on the vine. Look around you. It is not exactly Clapham Junction at rush hour, is it?'

Smee was glad of that. Not long before he had faced the horror of Clapham Junction at rush hour twice a day, and he hoped never to do it again. There was no denying that the turnout was sparse. He decided he would win back some of his lost points with the Professor by highlighting this paucity of interest to the vicar later in the day.

Mrs Potter stopped at their pew on her way to the front of the church. 'I'm so glad you gentlemen decided to join us,' she said.

'Hmph,' said the Professor. 'I suppose Smee has a point. It is helpful to understand one's enemy, and this outing to your church will serve to fuel our determination to rid the world of this kind of claptrap once and for all. And besides, it will be good research for my forthcoming series of children's books, particularly the one entitled "Your Parents Are Idiots", which will be aimed at children unfortunate enough to have been born into religious households. I have already written one called "Your Parents Are Correct", which is aimed at children fortunate enough to be raised by people who have read my books and agree with everything I say. All titles are forthcoming from HarperCollins which, as I am sure you are aware, is the noblest of the publishing houses.'

'Well, I do hope you enjoy the service. Oh, and Professor, I was wondering if you would consider giving a little talk to our discussion group afterwards? We have an occasional series called "Other Points of View", where people from different religions come along and chat to us about the sort of things they get up to. I know it's short notice, but if you could drop in and tell us all about what it's like to be a Humanoid that would be terrific.'

'… Ist, Mrs Potter,' sighed the Professor. 'Human*ist*.'

'I do apologise. I'll get the hang of it eventually. A few weeks ago we had a nice Sikh lady come along and talk to us, and she was ever so interesting. She told us all about their customs and the kinds of food they eat and why the men all wear turbans and so on. Would you think about it, Professor? We would be very grateful.'

'I had better consult my male secretary,' he said. 'Even though it is widely accepted that I have one of the sharpest minds of all time, I do often find that I am operating at such a high level that I need a Smee to help me with such mundane matters as arranging bookings and making sure my trousers are on the right way round. So what do you think, Smee? Could we fit this engagement into our schedule?'

'It would be an opportunity to give them what for, Professor,' said Smee. 'You could confront them with their idiocy and win them over to the Humanist cause.'

'Good thinking, Smee. It sounds as though it could be worthwhile. Now, ask her whether there is a fee attached.'

'Mrs Potter, the Professor was wondering what was on offer in the way of …'

'Tea and biscuits,' she said.

'Hmmm. I have worked for less. Earlier this year I gave a speech to a large auditorium filled with employees of the advertising agency Saatchi and Saatchi, and do you know how much I was paid for that?'

'No, Professor,' said Smee.

'Nothing. Not a sausage. I waived my appearance fee before they even had a chance to offer me one. It was an extraordinary privilege to be invited to stand before an audience comprised exclusively of people of extreme mental brilliance and unimpeachable integrity, and to request further remuneration would have been inappropriate. I wore a wonderful shirt and spoke to them about the difference between tin-openers and sharks, and there was a big screen with my head bouncing around all over it. It was all rather splendid.'

'I have seen the footage on the Internet,' Smee told Mrs Potter, 'and it was very impressive. Really cutting-edge stuff.'

'Tell Mrs Potter that I shall take very great pleasure in addressing her discussion group, and would you discreetly mention that my favourites are custard creams and Jammie Dodgers? Oh, and those pink wafer ones.'

'How super, Smee,' said Mrs Potter, before he had a chance to go through the charade of relaying the message. 'You tell the Professor that we have a variety pack, and he can have first choice. We meet in the Sunday School room straight after the service.' She darted away.

'They have a variety pack, Professor, and …'

'Yes, yes. I heard.'

To Smee's disappointment a stream of people arrived at the last minute and settled into their pews. The turnout ended up being quite respectable. The organist warmed up by playing a few bars of 'He Who Would Valiant Be', and Smee was close to saying that for all its faults the church had some decent tunes, but he decided against it; a decision he was glad of when the first hymn proper began, and the others rose to their feet. It was a dirge that neither man recognised. The congregation seemed familiar with it though and, led by the choir, they sang the dismal tune as heartily as they could.

As Reverend Potter took to the pulpit he sought out his house guests and gave them a friendly smile. 'Look at him, Smee,' snarled the Professor. 'Grinning at us like he thinks he's got us where he wants us. We'll wipe the smile off his face later on when we tell him what we thought of his sermon.'

As the service began, Smee looked around at the other people there, wondering what must be going through their minds. His heart thumped when he caught a glimpse of the woman from the Christmas lights event. Even though she was no longer dressed in black or wearing her headset, he recognised her right away. He was surprised and confused that her presence in church didn't make him like her any less.

Every once in a while he was able to see her through gaps between the worshippers as they knelt to pray or stood to sing. He wondered whether she would remember him, and he tried to work out what he could possibly say to her. He wished he had checked his hair in the mirror before leaving the house.

21

'And', thundered the Professor as he concluded his talk to the eleven members of the congregation who had come along to the impromptu meeting of the discussion group, 'I am unanimous in that.'

There was a round of applause, and Mrs Potter took the chair. 'Thank you, Professor,' she said. 'That was most illuminating; I'm sure we all now have a far clearer idea of what it means to be a ...' She looked at a piece of paper on which she had written the word, '... Humanist. Now, who has a question for our visitor?'

A man the Professor recognised as Cyril from the day before timorously raised his hand.

'Go ahead, Cyril,' said Mrs Potter.

'Hello Professor,' he began, nervously.

'We meet again. It seems a little cruel to ask, but I don't suppose there has been any improvement in that department?'

'Well, yes, as a matter of fact. The vicar told me I should pour some special liquid on it and move it around a bit, and I can't help thinking it's starting to do the trick.'

'You and he are deluded, Cyril. It is time to abandon all hope. Now what is your question?'

'Professor, you say that you believe in evolution and all

that, and it sounds very interesting, but I was wondering, if it's true then how come there aren't any hairy fish?'

Mrs Potter could see the Professor's eyes begin to bulge. She braced herself and listened once again to his impenetrable monologue. The moment it was finished, she moved the discussion along. 'I see Gladys has her hand up.'

'I agree with Cyril,' said Gladys. 'It does all sound very interesting. So you say that once this planet was just molten rocks, and now we're all here? You think that life just sprang from the ground? Isn't it amazing, if it's true? Speaking for myself, I happen to think that even if life did begin that way, then a certain gentleman by the name of God would have had something to do with it; but according to you, did a few atoms just bounce together one day and decide to become living things?'

'Oh, Gladys,' said the Professor, moving into fireside chat mode. 'Gladys, Gladys, Gladys. First of all there was nothing. Then the Big Bang came along, and the universe as we know it started, and it got bigger and bigger. And then, thousands of millions of years later, came life. If I were to attempt to put words to such a development, what could I do but fail? Even I, Professor Richard Dawkins, recipient of the 2002 Bicentennial Kelvin Medal of the Royal Philosophical Society of Glasgow, humbly accept that I would be mad – quite literally insane – to attempt words to do it justice. It is just too staggering to be conveyed by something as inadequate as language. Next question please.'

'I do hope you don't mind me pressing you, Professor,' said Gladys, 'but I wish you would at least *try* to tell us how you think life first came to be. It would be fascinating to hear, and it would really help us understand your beliefs.'

'How about this?' said the Professor. 'What if, a long time ago in a galaxy far, far away, a civilisation developed and through Darwinian means got so good at science that they were able to come to earth and plant little seeds of life; life which has, also through Darwinian means, evolved to where we are now?'

'So you're saying life was planted here by spacemen?'

'It is an intriguing possibility.'

'Like something out of *Doctor Who*?'

'*Exactly* like something out of *Doctor Who*. I am glad you understand me. At last I seem to be making some headway.'

Cyril chipped in. 'That nice Scientology lady said something similar when she came to talk to us, do you all remember?'

The members of the discussion group nodded at the memory. 'Yes, she was very nice, wasn't she?' said the head campanologist. 'It was a lot like what you're saying, Professor; something about spacemen jumping out of volcanoes. Isn't it funny how similar all world religions are once you scratch the surface? I always say we're praying to the same God in different ways. It's just you call God "science", and instead of Jesus you have Charles Darwin.'

The fireside chat was over. The Professor was white with fury. 'How dare you liken my movement to criminal organisations? You Anglicans, the Scientologists, the Methodists, Greek Orthodox, Hindus, you're all the same. It's a racket. In science we pray to no God because we have done the experiments that prove beyond doubt that He does not exist.'

'Just out of interest, Professor,' put in Mrs Potter, hoping to calm him down by returning to the question, 'who would you say invented these spacemen you've been telling us about?'

'They too would have developed by Darwinian means, of course.'

'From seeds planted by other spacemen?'

'I can see no reason why not.'

'Then who would have invented the first ever spaceman?'

'There are people working in that field who are making great strides towards answering such questions, but you can be assured that it is all entirely scientific and nothing whatsoever to do with religion. As I explained in my address, it is a simple fact that there is no God. Just because science cannot, at this moment, explain absolutely everything, there is no reason for you to disbelieve that everything is ultimately explicable. There is no excuse for you filling the gaps with mumbo-jumbo stories about bread, and floods, and colourful coats, and enchanted hair and so on. Look around you.' He pointed at pictures on the walls, drawn by Sunday School children. With Christmas coming up, most of these were nativity scenes. 'Magic stars, virgin births, angels, myrrh. It's all nonsense, all of it. None of that is real. Can you not see?'

'So you really don't know how life began?' said Gladys, genuinely fascinated and without a trace of accusation in her voice. 'How interesting. I thought you science people were all rather fussy about gathering evidence, but what you're doing here is guessing about spacemen. This is *such* an enlightening talk, Professor. And you told us earlier that Darwin's Theory of Evolution is a fact. Can you tell us, at what point does a theory become a fact?'

'When I say it does,' he hissed. 'I have done enough experiments for anything I say to count as science. How many experiments have *you* done? Nowhere near as many as me, that's how many. I strongly suggest you do as the alternative comedians do, and defer to somebody who knows an awful lot about science. And that somebody is me,' he pointed at himself, 'Professor Richard Dawkins.'

'It's a bit like Papal Infallibility, isn't it?' said Cyril. 'That nice Roman Catholic lady told us all about that, do you remember?' Everyone nodded at the memory. 'She said they believe that the Pope has special knowledge and they all go along with everything he says even though they might not entirely understand it.'

Smee was surprised to find that the Professor was not incensed at being compared to the pontiff; on the contrary, he responded quite calmly. 'We do not have a Pope figure in our movement; that would be contrary to our way of thinking. I do happen to be the most highly evolved of the bunch though, let's not pretend otherwise, and I suppose my extraordinary intellect allows me access to planes of understanding to which the others can never be party. Consequently they have a tendency to look up to me and, being a fairly bright bunch by and large, they accept everything I say as being absolutely correct.'

'It must be very gratifying that your Humanist friends have so much faith in you,' said Mrs Potter.

'Faith? What rot. They just recognise facts when they see them. And let me tell you this: to deny that the Theory of Evolution is a fact is tantamount to denying the Holocaust. If anything, there is more evidence for evolution than there is for the Holocaust.'

'Oh, Professor,' put in Mrs Potter, 'wouldn't you say that using such a dreadful episode to support your point is just a little on the tasteless side?'

'Tasteless? Pah. I shall tell you what is tasteless, Mrs Potter: questioning the plain truth that we are related to turnips. That is far more tasteless than making a clear and simple comparison with the slaughter of the Jewry. Any intelligent, informed and sane person can see that evolution, as described by Charles Darwin – that is *Darwin*, Mrs Potter, not that Chuzzlewit man – and improved upon by me, is a fact, and to question it on any level is a display of insanity on an intellectual par with the denial of the Holocaust. I am the sanest person I know, Mrs Potter. Just you remember that.'

'Well, I still think the comparison is rather unnecessary.'

'Pmph.'

The head campanologist raised his hand again. 'I heard something on Radio Four a few weeks ago about how there are lots of unknowns when it comes to evolution, and there's still a lot left to learn. They said that, as the years go by, palaeontologists are likely to make discoveries that contradict what is currently believed.'

'Yes, yes, of course,' he scoffed. 'These imaginary palaeontologists might even find a fossil of a Tooth Fairy, or a thing with forty eyes, or a perfectly preserved skeleton of a goblin with a purple face. They could even dig up a four-sided triangle; let us not rule out that possibility.'

'All they were saying was that, while there might be lots of facts within the Theory of Evolution, there are a lot of gaps too, so can we really say that it's unquestionably a fact?'

'Yes. And, as I stated earlier, I am unanimous in that. That you would even ask such a question suggests that your mind is unequal to the task of serious analysis. I have written books on the subject, you know. How many books have *you* written about it? Well? Come along, how many?'

'Er … none, I'm afraid.'

'As I thought, not a single one. And *you* would challenge *me*?' The Professor closed his eyes and shook his head. 'I know what you people need,' he said. 'I shall now show you something that will send you running from this church of yours, never to return. Smee, my apparatus.'

There was no answer.

'Smee?'

Smee's mind was elsewhere. After the church service the woman had walked past him, and had given him a smile of recognition and raised a hand in greeting. She still seemed really nice and, best of all, she had been there on her own. He had smiled back and raised his hand too.

'Smee?'

Smee jolted out of his daydream and realised he had missed his cue. 'Oh, yes, Professor. Of course. Your apparatus.' Smee opened a small hard case and took out the chemicals the Professor had prepared: a phial of potassium permanganate solution and a larger bottle containing a solution of sugar and sodium hydroxide.

Saying nothing, the Professor poured the contents of the bottle into a large beaker, swirled it around and, with a theatrical flourish, added the potassium permanganate.

There was a collective gasp as the liquid changed colour, a trick it repeated several times. When, after a few minutes, this display ended and the liquid went back to its original clear state, there was a round of applause.

'It is absolutely safe to say that anybody in this room who, after witnessing that experiment, still believes in God, is a fool. Now raise your hand if you still believe in God.'

Every member of the discussion group raised a hand.

'What?' cried the Professor. 'After what you just saw you still believe that there's a man in sky with a big beard who made you, and torments you, and judges you, and will condemn you to eternity in a burning pit just because he designed you in such a way that you could never be perfect?'

'It was a wonderful display, Professor,' said Cyril. 'It really reminded me of how amazing this world is, with all its chemicals and so on.'

'But you are Christians. You don't believe in chemicals, you believe in miracles.'

'Oh, Professor, everybody here believes in chemicals,' said Mrs Potter. 'If there really is a war raging between science and religion, there are no battles being fought in Market Horten. I'm sure everybody here, though we may not be experts by any means, holds science in high regard. Take Gladys, for example. She has just had a test-tube granddaughter, haven't you, Gladys?'

'I certainly have. And you would never know it. She looks just like a normal baby, and that's all thanks to science. In fact, I would say that even though I don't understand it, as a proud test-tube grandmother, I think that science is rather wonderful.'

'And for all I know there might even be something to your spaceman story,' said Mrs Potter, 'but if it is true then, just like Gladys, I believe that the guiding hand of God would have been behind it all.'

'Well, I don't.'

For a moment there was a quiet in the Sunday School room. Time seemed to stand still as the debate reached its inevitable impasse.

It was the Professor who spoke first. 'There is no reasoning with you people,' he huffed. 'If you still believe in miracles in the face of what you have just witnessed, then quite honestly you must have malfunctioning minds. It is the only conceivable explanation.'

'Just because something can be explained in scientific terms doesn't mean that it's not a miracle,' said Mrs Potter. 'I think that everything good is a miracle, whether it is explicable or not.'

'And what about all the bad things? What do you think about your beloved bearded ghost letting all those poor African children die left, right and centre? And what about athlete's foot? And haemorrhoids?'

'Sometimes it's the Devil,' said Gladys. 'God does the good things and the Devil does the bad things.'

'You people …' said the Professor, his eyes once more beginning to bulge. Then he sighed and shook his head. 'Sometimes I wonder why I bother trying to help you out. You know, my life would be so much easier if everybody was as clever as me.'

Mrs Potter decided that the time had come to wrap

up the discussion before things got out of hand. 'The Professor is a very busy man,' she said, 'and we mustn't keep him any longer. Thank you, Professor, for giving us such an interesting talk at short notice. It has been fascinating learning all about humanitarianism.'

'It's "Humanism", not "humanitarianism". Though I have to say that the two are not entirely dissimilar. There is something key to both of them, and that thing is niceness. To announce oneself as a Humanist is to hold aloft a placard which reads, "I am Intelligent, Rational and Nice".'

'I do apologise, Professor. It was certainly nice of you to come along today. Now let's all give him a clap.'

There was a short burst of applause and people started to wriggle back into their coats and scarves.

The Professor cleared his throat and made an announcement: 'Smee will pass among you now with some literature from the British Humanist Association. Once you have had a chance to absorb my talk, you will doubtless be impatient to join, and there are membership forms on the back page. The rates are very reasonable at thirty pounds a year, with a ten-pound discount for old-age pensioners. There is also a five-hundred-pound lifetime membership option, though I cannot see that making financial sense for many of you.'

Everybody politely took a flyer. When Smee had finished distributing them he returned to the Professor's side.

'I thought that went rather well, didn't you, Smee?'

There was no answer. Smee was gazing into the middle distance. A shaft of light was shining through the window and little bits of dust were dancing in the air. *Don't they look lovely?* he was thinking.

'Smee?'

'Oh, yes, Professor. You were wonderful.'

22

The Professor and Smee had joined the Potters for their Sunday roast.

'I'm afraid I heard some rather upsetting news about Old Aggie today,' the vicar told his wife. 'She's taken a turn for the worse. The doctor says she's unlikely to last a great deal longer.'

The Professor overheard this exchange and decided to join the conversation. 'Lucky her,' he said.

'She isn't lucky, Professor,' said Mrs Potter. 'She's gravely ill.'

'Of course she's lucky,' snapped the Professor. 'She's lucky that she was ever born. I have no idea who this Old Aggie character is, but I am sure she will not have the effrontery to complain as she stares death in the face. She will be grateful that she ever lived at all; chosen as she was like a single grain plucked at random from the ever-shifting sands of the Sahara desert.'

'It will be a terrible shame for her family when she goes,' sighed Mrs Potter. 'They are all so fond of her.'

'A terrible shame? Pfff. If her family cannot see the inevitability of her death and accept it for what it is then they must be fools. I have not heard from my third wife since Friday and for all I know she is lying in a lifeless heap on the kitchen floor. Do you see me crying about it? Well, do you?'

'Oh dear, Professor,' said Mrs Potter. 'Is she not picking up the phone?'

'No, as a matter of fact. I've tried her once or twice but to no avail. Anyway, it is her turn to call me.'

'Is there a neighbour who could check on her? It would put your mind at rest to know she's OK, wouldn't it?'

The Professor thought for a while. 'I suppose it would be something of a shame if she was to die without me by her side.'

'Of course it would, Professor.'

'I wouldn't be able to eat her, would I?'

'I beg your …? What was that, Professor?'

'I said, "I wouldn't be able to eat her."'

'Yes, I thought that was what I heard.'

'My third wife and I have a little agreement: if one of us is to become terminally ill we shall jet off to Papua New Guinea, where they are famously relaxed about that sort of thing, and when the final curtain falls the surviving spouse will feast heartily upon the corpse of the other. There will be no tears, just a lot of delicious food.'

'Isn't that all a little gory, Professor?'

'Gory? Good grief, it is the most natural thing in the world. I have no moral objection whatsoever to a little bit of cannibalism. We Humanists are all in favour of it; we have no room for sentimentality. Of course certain sections of the media like to distort this, calling us a "flesh-eating cult" and so on, but I can state quite categorically that we believe it is entirely wrong to kill people so we can eat them; they must always be dead in the first place. But no, there is no need to send anyone to check on her. If she has died it will be too late; whenever I'm away she always puts the central heating on full blast, and by now her body will be in an early state of decomposition, rendering her quite inedible. Unless …' The Professor scratched his chin. 'Unless she has collapsed and died in the garden, in which case the weather will have preserved her rather well. But no, the foxes will have got to her by now and besides, we have English law to contend with; I dare say some judge or other would have something to say about spousal consumption. Yet another example of the state interfering with the everyday activities of the supposedly private citizen. But no matter, the likelihood is that she remains extant. I blame her silence on the accursed telephone signal in this oversized village of yours.'

'You would be very welcome to use our home phone.'

'As I have explained, Mrs Potter, it is her turn to call me.'

'But she doesn't have our number, so if your phone is having trouble with incoming calls, how could she contact you? Oh, I do wish you would call her, Professor, or send somebody to check on her.'

'Possibly, in a day or two, but I honestly cannot

understand why you are making so much fuss. People die all the time. You two shan't be around a great deal longer, and even I am approaching an age when the Grim Reaper looms ever present. I mean that as a figure of speech, of course; despite what your holy book says there is no such person as the Grim Reaper. I cannot speak for Smee, as he is of indeterminate age, but there can be no doubt that the rest of us are entering the final furlong. I for one shall laugh in the face of death.'

'To return to Old Aggie,' said the vicar, 'she has asked for me. She is at home in the Bottoms. I'll do my best to reach her tomorrow. Let's hope the roads will have cleared enough to get through.'

'Why has she asked for you?' asked the Professor. 'What help could you possibly be?'

'I was her vicar for many years, and I suppose she would like to hear some words of consolation from a man of the cloth; and I shall of course say a prayer with her.'

'*Words of consolation*? *Say a prayer*? Oh, this is priceless! Did you hear all that, Smee? They really do talk like that, you know.'

Smee's mind snapped out of its latest daydream. 'You say you might be travelling to the Bottoms, Reverend?' he asked.

'Yes, Old Aggie lives in a hamlet called Back Bottom. It's so small it's not always marked on maps. The latest local weather forecast says there will be a slight thaw overnight, but they don't always get it right, do they?'

'*Don't always get it right*? Pshfff. Meteorology is science, and science is always correct. If my esteemed meteorological colleagues say there is going to be a thaw, then a thaw there shall be.'

'Let's hope you're right. The trouble is, it can be a bit of a tight squeeze getting into Back Bottom; the road there is tricky at the best of times; who knows what state it will be in tomorrow? Still, if I can get the four-wheel drive as far as Front Bottom I should be able to navigate the ridge that separates the two, on foot if need be. I have a good feeling that I shall get there somehow.'

'Reverend Potter,' said Smee, 'if it came to it, I wonder if you would have room for a couple of passengers? You see, the Professor is due to give a talk to the All Bottoms Women's Institute tomorrow at half past two. The last time I checked they were saying the train line was due to reopen this evening, but just in case it doesn't, I wonder if we might use you as a backup plan?'

'Well, I …'

Mrs Potter finished his answer for him. 'My husband would be delighted to take you up there, wouldn't you, dear?'

'Delighted? Would I? Really?' He sighed. 'If you say so, dear. Yes, Smee, I suppose you two can come along. But no infanticide, and no cannibalism. I shall be rather strict about that.'

'Thank you, Reverend,' said Smee. He felt a weight lift from his shoulders. He was going to get the Professor to the stage. Now he could stop worrying, and maybe even enjoy himself in Market Horten. He knew from the bus campaigns that not worrying and the enjoyment of life were the two central pillars of atheism, and he was nothing if not an atheist.

He wondered what the town would have in store for him on a cold Sunday evening.

23

Smee sat in the lounge bar of the George and Dragon with an empty plate and an empty pint glass in front of him. He caught a glimpse of himself in the mirror behind the optics and was reasonably pleased with what he saw. He had begun to worry that the Professor was right and that he had reached a point of life where his age had become indeterminate to disinterested observers, but he had combed his hair a certain way, and worn a certain shirt, and he was fairly sure his looks matched his years that night. He was thirty-nine.

He had come out alone on the pretext of fanning the flames of the debate that the Professor was sure was raging, in his favour, across the town. He had not spoken to anybody though, except the barman as he ordered pie and chips and a local ale. He checked one last time and she still wasn't there, so he put his coat and gloves back on and inched his way through the slippery streets to the next pub on his list.

A few minutes later he was sitting on a stool at the copper bar of the White Lion, taking the top off his second pint of the evening. Like the George and Dragon before it, the White Lion had a typically Sunday feel: there weren't very many people in, and the atmosphere was pleasantly subdued. A fire burned in the grate and he watched it, resisting the temptation to add a log or prod it with the poker. He opened a local free newspaper that had been left lying around, made his way through items about charity drives and parish council meetings, scanned the classifieds, and read reports of meetings of local history groups and previews of talks from naturalists. One piece announced a conjuring show for children that was due to take place at a community centre: 'featuring the magical Amazo the Amazing', it said.

Smee heard the Professor's voice in his mind: *Pfff. It is a disgrace, Smee. 'Magical' indeed. All this sort of nonsense does is tell children that magic is real, and from there it is easy to plant within their young minds the idea that miracles are possible. I shall dictate a letter to the nearest branch of the Humanists and tell them about this and they shall do as I say and stand outside the venue as the children leave, handing out leaflets telling them how these tricks are done. Each and every child must learn that magic is not real. They must be taught, with no room for doubt, that it is not the truth, that they are being lied to and that there is a scientific explanation for everything they saw.* He thought for a moment about tearing the page out and showing it to the Professor, and a few days earlier he would have done just that, but tonight he decided against it. He admitted to himself that he wanted the children to enjoy the show.

Every once in a while a voice would rise above the background hum, and he would tune in to a conversation that was happening elsewhere in the room. None of them seemed to be about infanticide. Groups of friends sat around tables, sharing bags of crisps and peanuts as they discussed the weather, and television programmes, and their lives and the lives of people they knew. Often some laughter would ring out. This was a world he had once been a part of and he had almost forgotten it existed. He knew the Professor was expecting him to introduce himself to these people, to sit alongside them and ask for their thoughts on his chosen topic, and go ballistic if they disagreed with him. He couldn't do it, though. It wasn't shyness; he had spent much of the preceding three weeks approaching strangers on the Professor's behalf and had become quite accustomed to it. Instead he found himself hamstrung by an overwhelming need to leave people alone, to let them get on with the evening without being caught up in a furious debate. He realised with a creeping sense of self-awareness that to approach them would make him a pub bore. And though he hated to admit it to himself, he wasn't 100 per cent sure that he agreed with the Professor's stance on infanticide.

He left the fire and conversation behind and went back into the cold, this time to the Wheatsheaf, a pleasant looking red-brick pub facing what must once have been the village green. The clear expanse was dotted with snowmen, and on the other side of it the silhouette of St Andrew's church was just visible in the orange glow of a streetlamp. A sign outside the pub said:

QUIZ TONIGHT
8.30 P.M.
PRIZES!

Smee checked his watch. It was eight twenty. This would be his last stop for the evening; if she wasn't there, she wasn't there. He pushed open the door, stepped inside and let the warmth embrace him.

24

Having suffered a stab of guilt at his abandonment of his stated mission to bring the Professor's findings and opinions into the Market Horten night, Smee had named his quiz team There Is No God. This way the Professor's rallying cry would be read out at the end of each round as the scores were announced. 'Never let them tell you that this is neither the time nor the place for such debate, Smee,' he had often said. 'This is an urgent struggle, and it is always the time and it is always the place.'

Smee's was the only team of one – not really a team at all. The others ranged from a middle-aged couple called The Lovebirds to an unwieldy and boisterous group of friends who had named themselves The Magnificent Eight. There were twelve teams in all, and results for round one were being announced. Smee, sitting at his small round table in the corner, cringed when the quizmaster announced that There Is No God was bringing up the rear, with just three points out of a possible ten. He tried to tell himself that his cringing was down to his poor performance and nothing to do with the name, but it didn't work. It had sprung from both sources.

He wished he had taken the whole night off from defending science from the onslaught of religion. He thought for a moment about bailing out, but he couldn't face going back to the Potters' so early in the evening. This was the first significant length of time he had spent away from the Professor since meeting him, and he tried not to admit to himself that he was glad of the respite. And besides, he was still holding out hope.

Round two began and Smee hunched over the answer sheet, willing the quizmaster to ask some kinder questions this time. His heart fell when the first was about sport: Which football team's ground is called Plainmoor? He was no expert when it came to football, but the more he thought about it the surer he became that this knowledge was buried somewhere in his mind. No matter how hard he scrabbled for it, it seemed just out of reach. And then the answer came to him.

A whisper in his ear: 'Torquay United.'

That was it. He knew it from his childhood holidays in Devon. He had even been to a match there once. He couldn't remember who Torquay United had been playing, or whether or not they had won, but he remembered standing on the terraces by his father's side as he watched the game. For a moment it was as if he could feel his dad's hand on his shoulder. Without daring to look up, he wrote 'Torquay United' on his answer sheet.

And then the voice said, 'Can I join your team?'

Smee found the courage he needed. He looked, and saw that it was her. He smiled. 'Please do. I need all the help I can get.'

She put her pint on the table and sat beside him. Before they had a chance to introduce themselves, the next question was read out, and as soon as they had finished grappling with that one, the next came along, and it wasn't until they had finished the round by listing every one of Top Cat's gang that they were finally able to begin something resembling a normal conversation. They were confident that they had scored at least eight out of ten. 'So what's our team name?' she asked, pen poised as she got ready to hand in their answer sheet.

Smee burned with embarrassment. 'There Is No God,' he mumbled.

'Pardon?'

He felt like machine-gunning himself in the head. 'There Is No God.'

'Really?'

'Really.'

'OK. I'd have gone for The Snowbound Outsider, or something like that. Serves me right for turning up late, doesn't it?' She smiled, and wrote 'There Is No God' at the top of the sheet, which she then took to the quizmaster for marking.

When she came back to the table she lined up two fresh pints. It was time for them to introduce themselves. 'Hello,' he said, extending his hand. 'I'm Smee.'

She shook it firmly. 'Smee?'

'Yes. Smee.'

'Is that Smee *something*, or *something* Smee?'

'Just Smee. It's very nice to meet you …'

'Catherine.'

Smee winced. 'C or K?'

'C.'

Smee winced again.

'Those were big winces. Ex-wife or ex-girlfriend?'

'Ex-wife.'

'And she always insisted on the full Catherine?'

Smee nodded.

'I do too, I'm afraid. I've tried the others, but they never seem right. I'm just not a Cathy or a Cat or a Katie.'

Smee winced again.

'You've heard all that before, haven't you? Just remember that I'm not her; I'm a completely different one.'

Smee wished he could tell her not to worry, that it had all been a long time ago, but it wouldn't have been true. She had left less than a year ago and legally they were still married. His life had been a shambles since she had gone; it wasn't until the Professor had rescued him that some semblance of structure had re-entered his days. 'We've been separated for a while now,' he said.

'If it's any consolation,' she said, 'I've got an ex who makes me pull that face too. But luckily for me he's not called Smee. Anyway, let's not talk about them. Let's have a nice time in the pub instead.'

'I'll drink to that,' said Smee, and they raised their glasses.

Before the conversation could go any further the quizmaster was back with the results of round two. There Is No God had done well, but so had lots of the other teams, and they had only risen to second from bottom. Round three began.

25

Aided by The Lovebirds, who had left before the final round, There Is No God finished in seventh place. In the micro conversations that had taken place between the questions, and in the short breaks between the rounds, Smee had found out a few things about his team mate.

She preferred real ale to lager.

She was staying upstairs at the pub until the roads were safe enough to get her little car out of town.

She had no idea where Bedfordshire was.

She had been stage-managing events for twelve years.

She had twice been stung by a wasp but never by a bee.

She had an eight-year-old daughter who was currently staying with her ex, who was the one not called Smee.

She knew every one of Top Cat's gang.

She had started a psychology course and was filling her time in Market Horten by reading textbooks.

She lived in a city about forty miles away.

She had never been to Germany.

She thought the Kinks were better than the Beatles.

She had once broken her arm.

Catherine had also found out some things about Smee.

He had never broken a bone.

He was fairly sure he had once eaten a mango.

He had lived alone in a rented studio flat since splitting with his wife at the start of the year.

He thought the Kinks were better than the Beatles.

He had been the Professor's assistant (he had chosen not to describe himself as a male secretary) for just over three weeks.

He was really called Michael Cartwright – not Mike or Mickey or Mick.

He could remember Benny the Ball but none of the others.

He liked real ale and lager about the same.

He had no children.

He had been to Germany.

He knew where Bedfordshire was, and had even lived there for four years in his late twenties.

They had another drink, to celebrate not having come

last. 'So,' said Smee, 'what did you think of the church service?'

'I liked it. I thought the sermon was really good. That vicar had some funny lines.'

Smee had to agree with her about Reverend Potter's humour; at points he had had trouble stifling laughter.

'I'd not been to church for years,' she said, 'but the landlady here is in the choir and she convinced me to go. I'm quite glad I did.'

'So you're not religious?'

'Not really. I sort of believe in God, but I think religion's a bit daft. I don't know, really. What I do know, though, is that there are a lot of weird things that nobody understands.'

Smee knew he ought to berate her for *sort of* believing in God. He heard the Professor's voice urging him on: *It is like 'sort of' believing in a goblin with a purple face. Mock her, Smee. Ridicule her. Ridicule her with contempt.*

He didn't want to ridicule her with contempt. He decided he wouldn't even pursue this line of conversation; he would rather talk about other things.

He was appreciating the opportunity to use normal language, without being berated for it. He was able to talk about the weather, rather than meteorological conditions, and instead of asking her whether she had consumed ample foodstuffs, he simply asked her whether she had already eaten. He only slipped up once, when he had said, 'Allow me to consult my chronometer,' but he had realised in time and was able to disguise this as a joke. Most of all he was enjoying having a conversation without it exploding.

The longer they spoke, the brighter the world became. It glided into focus in a way it hadn't for a long time. For months, until the Professor had come along, he had been a self-diagnosed depressive, a redundant divorcee-in-waiting who rarely left the house. He had spent his days hunched over his computer wearing makeshift pyjamas, and sometimes not even those, as he wrote comment after comment on Internet news sites.

He had been quite the expert on a range of topics: climate change; library closures; Iran's nuclear capability; infant nutrition; aspect ratios; press regulation; immigration; taxation; arts funding; assisted suicide; hacking; fracking; twerking; Pussy Riot; truancy; US fiscal policy; human rights; Vince Cable; free schools; Operation Yew Tree; vitamin pills; Katie Hopkins; drone strikes and, more than anything, religion. He specialised in an absolute conviction that there was no such thing as God and at the first opportunity he would launch assaults on anybody who was not as devoutly atheistic as he was. Orphaned, and now abandoned, he was at one with all the misery in the world. The idea of eternal life horrified him and he had been drawn, inexorably, to nothingness. He needed to know that one day there would be an end to the pain and, while he waited for that day to come, word bombs flew from his bedsit on to the Internet.

The pub quiz had shown him, though, that without broadband and access to a pile of back issues of *Prospect* magazine, he wasn't quite the fountain of knowledge he had believed himself to be. And with Catherine there, the world was no longer as bleak as it had seemed. She made him laugh and, even better than that, he made *her* laugh. He hadn't made anybody laugh for a very long time and he felt shivers every time it happened. His impersonation of Tecwen Whittock turned out to be just as amusing as it had been when it was topical and, as it reached its climax, she had had to wipe away a tear.

He thought of the life he had left behind and it seemed as if he was observing somebody he barely knew. He was embarrassed by all the humourless rage he had spewed on to the Internet. He recalled with a chill how he had gone through a phase of criticising other posters on news sites for their grammar. He had even started his final day of isolation by going to the *Independent* newspaper's website, finding a story in the Entertainment section and, without even reading it, writing underneath: 'Come along, Indie, is this really what passes for news in this day and age?' He had been the online equivalent of the pub bore, droning on as he put the world to rights. It was only then that he realised just how unwell he had been. Sitting across a pub table from Catherine, the anger and the isolation it had sprung from seemed as distant as Brazil.

The bell rang for last orders and they had another

drink. Disarmed by alcohol, he relaxed too much. He told her about how his life had been since his wife had gone away, about his adventures on the Internet and the way he had sometimes not dressed for days on end. She listened closely and, as he spoke, he could feel he was saying too much, but he carried on nonetheless. He tried to put a humorous, self-deprecating spin on it, but she didn't laugh. He could feel her slipping away as she looked at him with concern and, worse, pity.

26

As Smee walked through the icy streets back to the Potters' house, his head swam with beer and shame. He had been fooled into thinking that the universe had presented him with someone he could love, and who might love him in return. The evening had finished with an awkward exchange of numbers, the old-fashioned way, on pieces of paper that could so easily get lost.

Her pity had crushed him. It reminded him of the other Catherine. When she had left, it had been with such tenderness that he ended up wishing she could have been cruel and cold instead. There had been the unbearable visits to see how he was doing; the stream of unsolicited advice as it became apparent that he was not doing well; the Tupperware containers full of nutritious food that had arrived after she had seen the empty ready-meal boxes piled up on his kitchen floor; the way she had been so fair about the way their property was divided. If anything she had been *too* fair; he had wondered whether he could sense a whiff of charity. Worst of all had been the repeated assurances that there was nobody else. He hadn't been at all comforted to know that she would rather be with nobody at all than be with him.

A few weeks after the separation she had come to

visit him in his bedsit, as a patient is visited in hospital, and over a cup of tea she mentioned that she had made a new friend. 'He's called Laurence,' she said. 'He's a magician. I've told him all about you and he says he thinks you sound brilliant.'

Smee immediately discovered that knowing there was another man was immeasurably worse than straightforward abandonment, and that the only thing that had come between him and total collapse had been the hope of reconciliation. He hadn't been able to stop the tears and she had pulled out a handkerchief and passed it to him. It was vivid red and, as he took it, it became apparent that it was part of a long chain of similarly brightly coloured handkerchiefs that was emerging from her sleeve.

'Laurence has been teaching me some of his tricks,' she explained.

Through the haze he had heard her voice. 'Oh, poor you. Please don't cry, Michael. One day you'll meet the right girl.'

The next morning he had arranged to take voluntary redundancy from work and for the following months he had spent up to eighteen hours a day on the Internet, waiting for news articles to appear. When they did, he and a few other people, mainly separated men who had taken redundancy or were on long-term sick leave, would leave forceful comments below it, and within moments the original story would be forgotten as they bickered among themselves. Smee found comfort in this struggle. His powerlessness in every other aspect of his life was countered by the knowledge that the words he wrote were there to be read across the world. As he typed away he was able to convince himself that he was doing something worthwhile, that the world needed to hear his opinions, that he was somehow making a difference.

Then would come the moments of clarity, when he saw what he had become. The piles of plastic and cardboard; the sheets that hadn't been washed for weeks; the lump sum, that had seemed so substantial when it had arrived, shrinking faster than seemed fair. All of this was horribly underpinned by a relentless and terrifying flaccidity. Unable to bear it, he would retreat from this clarity and return to the battle.

He fell three times on the ice and by the time he got back to the room he had a collection of bruises and a sprain. The Professor was fast asleep. Smee kicked off his boots, took off some of his clothes, lay down and pulled the duvet over himself.

His roommate stirred, rolled over and grunted before loudly declaring, 'There is no God. No God at all.'

Smee was ashamed at having allowed himself to wander into the wilderness. The Professor had saved him once and he would save him again. He knew his place in the world, and it was at the Professor's right hand, doing his bidding.

27

There had been no thaw, and a layer of fresh snow had fallen overnight.

'So much for meteorology,' said the vicar, taking the top off his egg.

'Pssshh. So much for prayer,' retorted the Professor. 'I would wager a pound to a penny that you implored that God of yours to melt the ice and clear the road to Old Aggie's.'

'I must admit to having put in a polite request to the Holy Ghost.'

'You were talking to yourself, you know. You would have done better to ask a lamppost to help you out; at least a lamppost exists.'

'It seems neither of us can claim victory. Let's call this one a draw.'

'Well, *I* shall be heading to the Bottoms,' said the Professor. 'Smee has assured me that he will get me there, and I have no reason to doubt him. He is upstairs now, making final preparations.'

'I hear the train line is open again,' said Mrs Potter, 'so I'm sure your talk will go ahead.'

The Reverend smiled at this. With his speech given,

the Professor would return to their house for a final night before moving to a new town, leaving the people of Market Horten, in particular its semi-retired vicars, in peace. Old Aggie lived a long way from her nearest railway station though, so he was left with the problem of getting there on treacherous roads. He held out hope that they would just about be clear enough.

'Now, Professor,' said Mrs Potter. 'I am going to ask you to promise me something.'

'Promise you? Pffff. Promises are for the weak, for the religious. I shall promise nothing.'

'Then will you make an agreement with me?' she asked.

'What sort of agreement?'

'A scientific agreement.'

'Now *that* I am open to, Mrs Potter. Do you see how each day you are drawn ever closer to my way of thinking? I do believe that the light of rational thought is beginning to shine in those blue eyes of yours. Now what would you like this scientific agreement to be about?'

'Would you please scientifically agree to call your wife? I could hardly sleep last night for worrying about her.'

'But I have an important speech to prepare. I cannot be distracted by such foolishness.'

'Please, Professor.'

'Absolutely not. And I am unanimous in that.'

'Then straight after the speech, will you give her a call? And if she doesn't answer, would you send someone round to check on her? I'm ever so worried about her, you see. The weather is atrocious, and she might be in difficulty.'

'Hmph. I suppose I could scientifically agree to that, and make some cursory attempt at contact once my obligations have been discharged.'

'That is a relief. Thank you, Professor.'

She left the room and Smee came in, looking pale. 'I have two pieces of news, Professor, neither particularly uplifting, I am afraid to say.'

'Continue.'

'I am sorry to report that your talk to the nursery school science club, which had been scheduled to take place this coming Wednesday, has been called off.'

'The snow again, Smee. Honestly, this country. One snowflake falls, and ...'

'I'm afraid it's not the snow this time, Professor. The learning-through-play coordinator contacted me to say that because they haven't received the necessary paperwork for your background check in time, they will be unable to let you on to the premises.'

'In case I am a child molester.'

'I'm afraid so.'

'Yet another thing that is wrong with this country: everybody is considered a child molester until proven otherwise. Well, let me tell you this, Smee: I was one of the instigators of the HAM movement, Humanists Against Molestation. It was set up in reaction to the incessant stream of allegations coming from various of the Christian churches. Including, vicar, your own.'

'The church has been through some dark times recently, that is true.'

'We atheists simply aren't interested in that sort of thing; there has never been an atheist child molester. So the booking has slipped through our fingers, Smee. I was planning on dissecting a puppy for those children, so they could find out how their pets work. Young minds which would have been brought to life by science will remain in the dark, susceptible to influence from the dark forces of religion. You do realise, of course, that this makes my journey to Upper Bottom all the more pressing. With so much to fight against, it is imperative that I let those women know how wrong, how very wrong, they are. And here is the best part, Smee: the Women's Institute is entirely secular. Though largely comprised of churchgoers, it is not tied to any religious organisation, so even with all its members converted to Humanism, the All Bottoms Women's Institute shall remain. We shall be able to maintain its infrastructure and from there, one by one, the branches will fall like dominoes. Each and every one will come over to our side until we have a female atheist battalion in every community in the land. I have it all planned out, Smee. This country is under siege from religion, and it must be saved. Cometh the hour, cometh the Professor, and that Professor is me, Professor Richard Dawkins. There is no question, Smee, that this will be the most important speech of my life. Now, what is the other item of bad news?'

Smee gulped. 'The train line is closed again, Professor. There's been an avalanche, which will take all day to clear. And they say the main road to the Bottoms is covered in black ice. Travel is not advised under any circumstances.'

The vicar rubbed his forehead, but the Professor did not seem perturbed. 'That is not something for me to worry about, is it Smee?' he said.

'Is it not?'

'No, because you have assured me that you will get me to my talk. You will find a way. And if you do not ...' He held a palm out flat, then very slowly balled it into a fist while making a chilling crunching sound.

'Yes, Professor,' gulped Smee. He left the room even paler than when he had come in.

Silences between the vicar and the Professor had become something of a tradition, but Reverend Potter found them even more exhausting than conversation, and he decided to try and beat this one before it happened. 'So how did you two boys meet?' he asked.

'My previous Smee was leaving to take up a prominent role somewhere, I can't remember where exactly; usually it's the BBC, or the *Guardian*, or the Labour Party or thereabouts. I asked her – this was a lady Smee, you understand – to find me a successor. She went on to that Internet thing, and showed me a comment under one of the latest news stories. It was around the time of that fascinating typhoon in the Philippines; did you hear about that?'

'Oh yes, it was terrible. We held a fund-raising coffee morning straight away.'

'Somebody had written under the article: "I wonder how the Christians are going to explain this one away: thousands dead, millions displaced. Their so-called 'God' is certainly moving in mysterious ways today." Sometimes I despair of the human race, but when I read words of such quality, subtlety and wisdom it makes me feel that I am not alone in my endeavours. I told my then Smee that our search was over. She contacted him and he ran to me immediately, as they always do, and started as my male secretary that same day.'

A car's horn sounded outside and the Professor and the vicar looked through the window. A light grey car sat outside. On its side, in large blue letters, was written: 'Dave's Taxi'.

Smee came back into the room. 'Coat on, Professor,' he said. 'We are off to the Bottoms.'

28

'I'm telling you, boys, you're barking up the wrong tree,' said Dave, driving slowly along the newly gritted road. 'First off, there's no way I can take you up the Bottoms today because there's big hills between here and there, and the road's covered in ice; and second off, you're directing me the wrong way. Even if the Bottoms *weren't* blocked, they're back that way, not down this way.'

'Trust me, Dave,' said Smee. 'I know what I'm doing'

'Hmph,' said the Professor. 'Smee, your future as my male secretary is now hanging by a thread so thin that, were it not figurative, one would require a special microscope to see it.'

The thread again. Smee told himself he was absolutely confident that his plan would work. The talk would go ahead and the figurative thread would once again become visible to the naked eye.

Smee issued a few more directions and, when they started down a dead end with only one possible destination, Dave realised where they were going. 'Hang on a sec,' he said. 'Let me think of a method of contact and an alliterating vegetable.' A few moments passed and he said, 'Clonk me with a carrot! You're taking us to the army base.'

'Base?' snapped the Professor. 'Why are we going to an army base?'

'Because our original plans fell through. As you say, Professor, needs must when the Devil drives. When the military find out that they have been graced with the presence of our land's most distinguished academic, and realise that members of the Women's Institute, the very backbone of our nation, are waiting for him, they will be sure to mobilise a helicopter and get us to Upper Bottom in time for a pub lunch before we amble over to the village hall for your talk.'

'Smee,' said the Professor, 'you might just have saved your bacon.'

29

The men were not allowed into the base and had been ushered into a small reception cabin outside the main gate. 'Gentlemen,' boomed the sergeant major, across the counter, 'you all seem like lovely boys but, in a word, *no*. We are not going to mobilise a helicopter just so you can give a talk at a village hall. It's hardly a matter of life or death.'

'Remind him who I am, Smee,' said the Professor.

'I remember who you are, Professor. It was less than a minute ago that your friend here was telling me all about your prizes and your books: *The Extended* … What was it?'

'Tell him, Smee.'

'*Phenotype*, Sergeant Major.'

'It sounds like a fascinating read, and I shall certainly put it on my list. Please don't take it personally, Professor. Even if a *really* famous scientist – Brian Cox, say, or David Bellamy – was to walk in here now asking to be given a ride up the Bottoms, we still wouldn't oblige. We would bring them a nice cup of tea and tell them how much we've enjoyed watching their programmes, and maybe even ask for signed photographs, but that would be all. No helicopter.'

'We had thought that if Mr Tumble could get access to one,' attempted Smee, in desperation, 'then perhaps we might too.'

The sergeant major went quiet and looked very serious. His eyes darted left and right and he leaned forward, making it clear that they were speaking in confidence. 'There is only so much I am at liberty to say about Operation Tumble,' he said, his voice low. 'Let's just say he has contacts high up in the military, and leave it at that. *Very* high up. And I shouldn't be telling you this because it's top secret information, but the helicopter hasn't flown since that night. Even if Sir David Attenborough himself was to come here in pursuit of the mighty golden eagle we wouldn't be able to fly him anywhere because we haven't got anything to fly him with. It's being fixed.'

'What's wrong with it?' asked Dave.

'I think it needs a new spinner thing. What's that called?'

'Rotor blade?'

'That's it. It won't be back in action until Wednesday. You can't fly a 'copter without its spinner.'

'Wednesday?' roared the Professor. 'What if war breaks out?'

'I hadn't really thought about that. I suppose we'll just have to make do with what we've got.'

The receptionist came through with the hot drinks that Smee, Dave and the Professor had been offered on their arrival. They sat in silence. Smee knew he had lost. This had been his final throw of the dice. In a day or two he would be back in his bedsit, curtains drawn and nothing but unlimited broadband and microwaved ready meals for company. It was what he deserved. The Professor had given him a chance of another life, a better life, but he had blown it.

The cabin door opened and a gust of icy air blew in. The three men looked over to see who had arrived. 'Look,' said the Professor, his voice reverberating around the room, 'it's that vicar whose house we're staying at.'

Being only a few feet away, Reverend Potter heard this. He turned and saw the three men. 'Hello Dave,' he said. 'Hello Smee. The Professor too. What a treat.'

30

'We don't have a working helicopter at the moment, vicar,' said the sergeant major, gravely, upon hearing the news that Old Aggie was in a bad way, 'but don't worry, we'll get you to her bedside.'

'That is such a relief. I felt so helpless sitting at home, knowing she was asking for me.'

'Did you hear that, Smee?' whispered the Professor, as he eavesdropped. 'As ever, there is one rule for world-renowned evolutionary biologists, and quite another for those who openly believe in supernatural balderdash. This is a little glimpse into how the world works – the war machine and the clergy, cheek by jowl.'

'There's just one thing,' said the Reverend. 'I'm afraid I shall be in trouble with my wife if she hears that I ran into the Professor and didn't at least *ask* if they could come along too. You see, he has a little talk to give …'

The sergeant major finished the vicar's sentence for him. '… At the village hall in Upper Bottom, at half past two. Well,' he sighed, 'it wouldn't be too far out of our way. And the Women's Institute *is* the backbone of our nation. I suppose we could fit it in and call it a round trip.'

'That is very good of you,' said the vicar, trying hard not

to look disappointed that his request had been granted.

'Let me arrange the transportation,' said the sergeant major. He picked up the phone and passed on some indecipherable coded messages. Smee had never felt more relieved; it seemed he had sidestepped his downfall once again. The ready meals would have to wait.

A few minutes later, they heard the throaty throb of a large engine outside the cabin. 'I shall accompany you, gents,' said the sergeant major. 'It's been a while since I saw Old Aggie, and I would like to pay my respects.'

Reverend Potter, Smee and the Professor followed the sergeant major out of the cabin. And there, waiting for them, was a green army tank.

Dave looked on as the men, aided by a pair of soldiers, clambered up on to it and disappeared down the hatch. 'Now then,' he said to himself as the tank moved off, its cannon pointing the way and its caterpillar tracks leaving a clear impression behind it as it packed down the snow under its extraordinary weight. 'Let me think.' He watched until it rounded a bend and disappeared from view and, even when it was gone, he kept on looking. 'You can … er … feel me with some fennel.' He knew it wasn't one of his stronger ones, but he wasn't too hard on himself. He thought he had done quite well to find any words at all.

31

'When faced with somebody like you, Sergeant Major,' said the Professor, 'I have been known to quote the award-winning journalist Johann Hari, who says, simply, "I have so much respect for you that I cannot respect your ridiculous ideas." I have recently modified this, however, to: "I respect you too much to accept that you really believe anything so ridiculous as you claim. Please either defend those beliefs and explain why they are not ridiculous, or else declare that you do not hold them and publicly disown the church to which you claim loyalty." With no offence meant to dear Johann, I am sure you will agree that my version is far snappier. As Smee will attest, I am not one to tickle my own ivories but it is no wonder that I was chosen for the inaugural Simonyi Professorship for the Public Understanding of Science; there are few who connect with the lay person as expertly as I. When I speak, I speak to all: from commoner to king, from peasant to, as we see now, soldier. I believe the thesis of Hari's original draft remains in my modified version, and I invite you to contest it, but beware: to do so would be to challenge not only the man himself, but also the committee of the 2008 Orwell Prize, who bestowed upon him one of journalism's highest honours.

Ask yourself, Sergeant Major, would you have the intellectual capacity to take on such men and, indeed, women? Let us not forget the ladies. You will find no greater supporter of women's rights than me.' He pointed at himself. 'Professor Richard Dawkins. Not like our friend the Mohammedan, although of course we are not allowed to say that sort of thing these days, are we? Well, I shall say it anyway, and hang the consequences. There are some who would call me intolerant for saying so, but those people are wrong. You will have to travel a long way to find anybody more tolerant than me. Just the other day I saw a lady who was quite openly chewing gum, and do you know what I did? I tolerated her. And then along came a young man in a backwards baseball cap, and what did I do? I tolerated him as well. Tolerance – that is my watchword: tolerance, tolerance, tolerance. And while we are on the subject …'

The roar of the engine had prevented the sergeant major from hearing a word the Professor was saying. He turned to the vicar, who was sitting beside him, and bellowed in his ear, 'What do you think he's on about?'

The vicar shouted back. 'He's probably saying that God doesn't exist and that science has all the answers, and that anybody who is religious must be a little soft in the head.'

'He's one of those, is he?'

'Very much so. He does go on.'

'He asked me if I believed in God as we were getting

into the tank. It's quite a rude question, really. It's none of his business, but I don't see why I should cover it up.'

'Let's just leave him to it.'

They watched the Professor for a while longer, as he stabbed the air with a forefinger to add emphasis to his unheard points.

'Does he ever shut up?'

'He'll sulk from time to time, but by and large this is what you get. It's a shame, really. I've read up on him and he has some fascinating ideas buried under all the bluster; he's certainly a dab hand at the awkward question. There's something of the John Wesley about him in his devotion to his ministry, but I don't suppose even Wesley would ever have been quite so strident. It's all rather off-putting.'

The Professor noticed this breakaway conversation and leaned forward to loudly request that he exchange places with the vicar. 'I think I would better get my point across were I to sit beside the man,' he shouted.

Through the medium of facial expression, the vicar did his best to express his discouragement of this development.

'Oh, let him,' said the sergeant major.

The vicar, telling himself that it wouldn't be *too* long a journey, exchanged places with the Professor.

Smee and the vicar sat opposite the Professor and the sergeant major, watching what appeared to be a rather one-sided conversation. At first the sergeant major seemed to be contributing the occasional 'I see' or 'If you say so', but soon these stopped and he fell silent. His lips turned white and the rest of his face blazed red. His eyes burned and, finally, inevitably, in a way that reminded both Smee and the vicar of popcorn, he exploded. In a voice so loud that it was plainly audible over the engine, he roared, 'You 'orrible little man. Consider yourself court-martialled and dishonourably discharged.' He signalled to the driver, who switched off the engine. 'Now get out of my tank.'

The silence came with a ringing in the ears. All eyes were on the Professor, to see how he would take this order.

'Very well,' he said. 'If that is how you feel, I would not wish to remain, in any case. Smee, we are leaving.'

'The boy can stay,' said the sergeant major. 'If he so chooses.'

'Smee,' repeated the Professor, 'we are leaving.'

All eyes were now on Smee.

32

The Professor stood in the snow, watching the tank as it continued without him up a narrow country lane. 'So what do you propose we do now, Smee?' he asked. The air was freezing and a breeze bit through their many layers of clothing. 'You got us into this mess; now let's see you get us out of it.'

Smee's feet had gone beyond numbness and come out the other side. They started to hurt, as if they were being sliced. He checked his phone. There was no signal. 'We need to keep moving, Professor. If we remain still we shall freeze.'

'Then I suppose we must follow the tank tracks back to the base.'

'No, Professor. We shall follow the tank tracks the other way. Old Aggie lives in the direction of Upper Bottom, so we shall at least be heading the right way. I told you I would get you to your talk, and get you there I shall.' He looked at his watch. 'We still have almost three hours.'

'Spoken like a true Englishman, Smee. Onwards.'

They walked on, in the bright light and quiet of the lane. On either side were fields covered in virgin snow. Smee felt an urge to run into them and make footprints and roll a giant snowball, but he knew that this was not the time. The idyll didn't last long, as misgivings began to creep in. He asked himself whether he had made the right decision in continuing. The movement of his body had not had a noticeably positive effect on his feet, and it had become quite an effort to put one in front of the other. It didn't help that the adrenaline that had propelled him this far into the day was wearing off. The beer and bruises from the night before were starting to make their presence felt, and he was weighed down by the bag they had packed for their outing. He had brought the Professor's chemicals, but he had not brought any food.

He wasn't sure where they were, or how far they had gone, or how far they had left to go, but he carried on. He could see no alternative.

Just as he felt that exhaustion and frostbite were imminent possibilities, he heard something. It was unmistakably the sound of an approaching vehicle. It grew louder and louder and eventually came into view. It was a Land Rover and on the side, in lurid green stencilling, were the words: ONE LIFE – LIVE IT.

'Now here is a gentleman after my own heart,' said the Professor, spotting the slogan. 'A philosopher. I may even appropriate his motto for the title of my next book; though I dare say Grayling would come out with a volume of his own six months later, called "Live Your One Life" or somesuch. Flag our new friend down, Smee.'

The Land Rover did not need to be flagged down; the

driver pulled over anyway. A giant of a man with a thick beard and woolly hat leaned out of the window. 'What are you boys up to?' He didn't wait for an answer. 'Hop in,' he said.

A collie was on the passenger seat, so the Professor and Smee got into the back.

'I am rather taken with your slogan,' said the Professor. 'I, for one, bound from my bed every morning, eager to find out as much as I can about this world in which we are living for such a short time. I hold the slugabed in low esteem. I believe you and I to be kindred spirits. I mean that as a figure of speech, of course. You know as well as I do that there are no such things as spirits.'

'There's whisky,' joked the man. 'I'll be having some of that when I get home. But it's not my Land Rover,' he said. 'It's my brother's. To be honest, I'm a bit embarrassed by that slogan.' The man eased the vehicle back into motion.

'But I am sure you broadly support the message,' said the Professor. 'Isn't it wonderful to not believe in God?'

'I think there's been a mix up. As I said, it's my brother who put that slogan there, not me. I *do* believe in God. Very much so, as a matter of fact. I didn't used to, but one or two things happened in my life that got me thinking.'

The Professor laughed and slapped his thigh. 'You mean you actually believe in all that nonsense?'

Oh no, thought Smee. *Here we go again.*

33

Even in a vehicle built for harsh terrain, progress was slow. They hadn't gone very far at all when the bearded man stopped, pulled up the handbrake and switched off the engine. He stared at the steering wheel and spoke in a voice little more than a whisper. 'I don't know who you are, and I don't know why you thought it would be a good idea to speak to me like that, but let me tell you something.' He turned around and looked directly at the Professor. Now his voice was almost deafening. 'I have killed a man. I have killed with these hands.' He held them up. Smee was sure they were the largest hands he had ever seen. They were heavily scarred and ingrained with dirt. 'And I don't want to kill again. I don't want to go back inside. But I can feel my blood boiling and, for your own good as well as mine, you had better get out while you still have a chance.'

The discussion had not gone well.

'It would appear that neither rational thought nor home truths are welcome in this vehicle, Smee. Come along, out we get.'

'*You* can stay,' the man said, pointing one of his vast fingers at Smee. 'I haven't got a problem with you. You can thaw out by my log fire, my friend.'

For a moment Smee was tempted to take up this offer and leave the Professor to his fate. But he remembered Catherine and he recalled her look of pity, and he knew that above all he must not be pitiable. Nothing would be more pitiable than failing to stand up for what he believed in, and he reminded himself that he believed in the Professor. He left behind the possibility of warmth in a self-confessed killer's isolated bothy and again went with the Professor into the snow.

The man restarted his engine, leaned out of the window, gave Smee a final chance to get back in, then pointed at the Professor and called him a bell-end before driving away.

Once again the men were alone in the snow. They watched the Land Rover until it rounded a bend.

'A bell-end, Smee,' the Professor sighed. 'All I am doing is trying to help, and they call me a bell-end.'

Smee had heard the Professor be called lots of names over the course of the preceding three weeks. *Bell-end*, *twat* and *dickhead* were the ones which arose with the most frequency. Although familiar with *twat* and *dickhead*, the Professor had not come across *bell-end* before, and had at first believed it to be a high compliment. He had responded graciously whenever it was thrown at him, and he had not learned its true meaning until somebody had taken out a pad of paper and illustrated his insult, with the word YOU written alongside it and an arrow pointing to the anatomical part in question.

The Land Rover reappeared, in reverse. Smee supposed the Professor had antagonised the driver so much that he was coming back to kill him anyway. He tried to ready himself to do what he could to defuse the situation.

When he got to them, the driver leaned out of the window. 'I'm sorry,' he said. 'You're entitled to your opinions. And if I leave you here you'll probably die of the cold, so it would be the same as killing you. I promised my prison chaplain I would never kill again and I don't want to let him down.'

'Hmph,' said the Professor. 'You only don't want to kill me because you are frightened of what your God would do to punish you, and that is just pathetic. I, on the other hand, would not kill because it is against my moral code, which I have developed to a very high degree without recourse to anything as silly as scripture.'

'Jump in, anyway,' the man sighed. 'Let's get you to wherever it is you're going. I never really had a chance to ask before.'

'Very well. You may take us to the village hall in Upper Bottom. In we get, Smee. Let us allow the poor man to think he is earning some heaven points by sparing our lives and delivering us to our destination.'

The Professor and Smee got back into the Land Rover, which drove away. Two minutes later it stopped again and out stepped the Professor and Smee. There had been another discussion, which had gone even worse than the first one.

'Wait,' the man said. He opened the glove compartment and, after some rattling, slammed it shut. Smee looked on in fear as a giant hand reached through the open window. He was relieved to see he wasn't holding a gun. He threw a small packet to Smee. A quarter of a bar of Kendal Mint Cake.

'Thank you,' said Smee.

The man pointed at the Professor and called him a wazzock, which was a first as far as Smee knew. He explained that if he kicked them out into the snow, at least they would have a *chance* of survival. 'And for the record,' he said, 'if there's one thing I learned in eighteen years of confinement, it's that anybody who invokes the Holocaust as a way of propping up their arguments is a desperate twat.' He drove away. Soon he was gone from view and the sound of his engine could not be heard.

'So this is how it ends, Smee. Cast out by the followers of Christ. For a long while I have been curious to discover how it must feel to be at the very end of life. Let us now find out, as we recline by the roadside in beds of everlasting snow.'

He lay down on the verge to die, and Smee lay down beside him.

34

The breeze had stopped. The sky was clear blue, and Smee looked up at it. With every exhalation came a small cloud; he wondered how many more of these there would be before hypothermia claimed him.

His mind jumped around. For a flash he was a child again, then he was at his mother's deathbed, then standing at the altar on his wedding day, and next he was inside an episode of *The Magic Roundabout*, then back amid the squalor of the tiny flat he had left behind. And then she appeared: the woman in black. She was telling him to get up, not to let the snow claim him. She wasn't angry, but she was exasperated. *Michael*, she was saying. *Michael, get up. I gave you my phone number because I want you to call me. If you die in the snow, it will have been a complete waste of paper.*

He remembered a feeling from the night before. It was something physical that had eluded him for months. It was basic biology and, at the thought of her, this feeling returned, even in the cold of the snow. Urged on by this reason to live, he sprang to his feet. 'Professor, we are not giving up.'

'Smee, I can barely move or draw my breath. Let me freeze to death.'

'No, Professor. I strongly believe that we have been premature in deciding to die in the snow. We must continue. To give up now would be to let them win, to hand victory to those who would silence you. And let us remember, we are British.'

'But think about it, Smee. What could be more British than dying in the snow? The time is upon us. They shall all come to my memorial service, of course, and what a secular occasion it will be. I can picture it now, everybody filing in with solemn faces: Fry; Curtis; Moffat; Rusbridger; McEwan; all the alternative comedians; that ghastly little Irishman with the sunglasses who always turns up at funerals.' His eyes were still, seeming to see nothing. 'The best of all, Smee, is … The best of all is that …' The cold genius's voice faded to nothing and his eyes closed.

'Would some Kendal Mint Cake help?'

'Ugh,' he said, weakly. 'It is like eating solidified toothpaste. I would sooner die, Smee. But wait.' His eyes snapped open. 'Where is my honey? I take a jar of honey with me everywhere I go. Maybe that will revive me.' He looked around.

'I'm afraid your jar of honey was confiscated at an airport a few weeks ago,' said Smee, who had heard the Professor furiously recount the story several times.

'Of course,' he whispered. 'I was forgetting for a moment that Bin Laden had won. He might as well be here now, administering the death blow.'

Smee heard something cut through the silence like a hoarse bluebottle. It was another engine. It was getting closer. 'Professor, I am going to be strict with you now. If we are to be rescued again we must have no debate on the subjects of science and religion. Do you understand?'

'Oh, let me die, Smee.'

The Professor's eyes closed and his breathing became shallow. The bluebottle's buzz became a rumble then a roar: the tank had returned. The hatch opened and the vicar's head emerged. 'We've come to a decision,' he said. 'We can't have you two freezing to death, so you can come along with us. You're just not allowed inside; you have to stay on top of the gun turret. Not you, Smee. You can come in, if you want.'

The Professor seemed not to have noticed any of this happening. 'Can you hear that, Smee? It's the music from the Hovis advert, I am sure of it. It is so calming. I am quite transported. And look: is that a rainbow, or is it a bridge? Perhaps it is both ...'

Smee could hear no music and see no rainbow. He held out his hand. The Professor took it, and he used all his strength to lift the enfeebled old man to his feet. It was quite an effort to help him into place on the gun turret, and he chose to stay outside with him. He knocked on the metal hatch and the tank moved off.

They made their way along the track towards Old Aggie's house. After a few minutes the Professor's vigour returned and he started running through his planned speech as if nothing unusual had happened. 'I shall undermine all the old certainties of the good ladies of the Bottoms,' he raged. 'They shall leave the village hall new people, as if they had been born for a second time. They will be ready to stand up for science and for reason, eager to passionately denounce the scourge that is called "religion", in all its guises. You know, Smee, I feel quite refreshed. Regenerated, even. Tell me, do I look different? A little like Peter Capaldi, perhaps?'

'I'm afraid not, Professor.'

'One day it will happen,' he said, then he launched back into his rehearsal. As the Professor carried on, Smee noticed a sign saying FRONT BOTTOM and they passed through a tiny hamlet. From what he remembered there was just a short ridge between there and Back Bottom. Sure enough, after a couple of minutes, a small cluster of houses appeared. They passed the houses and made their way along a track with a farmhouse at the end.

The Professor rose to his feet. 'No more shall those proud women accept the poison they have been spoon-fed from the cradle. No more shall they …'

A dog ran out in front of the tank, barking at the unusual sight. The driver braked sharply. Smee slid forward and managed to get a grip on the cannon, but the Professor had nothing to hold on to. Smee watched, helpless, as he was thrown from the tank and flew, head first, towards the hard ground.

The earth had been frozen for days. Smee knew that

even with a coating of snow on top, the impact would be similar to landing hard and fast on a concrete surface. The Professor was not in a good position for landing: his arms were by his sides as he fell, but when his head hit the ground something unexpected happened.

The earth seemed not to stop him. A human javelin, he ploughed through the snow and just kept on going. And then he was gone. There was a small hole at the point where he had passed into the ground, and then this closed in on itself. He had been swallowed up.

35

The hatch opened and the vicar and the sergeant major came out.

'Smee, are you all right?' asked the vicar.

'I'm fine,' he said, disentangling himself from the big gun. 'But the Professor's disappeared.' He pointed at the spot where he had seen him vanish. Just as he did, the snow began to move, and from underground there arose a strange brown monster. It climbed out of the ground and stood up, with steam rising from its body. From amid the brownness, eyes like the eyes of a human opened and looked up at the men on the tank. Next the beast's mouth opened, and it let out a fearsome roar that rang through the silent countryside:

'In the name of all that is secular, this will not do.'

'It's the Professor!' cried Smee. 'He's alive.' The men rushed down to greet the brown monster.

'It's a miracle,' said the sergeant major. 'He landed in Old Aggie's slurry pit. It must have still been soft under the surface.'

'Of course,' said the Professor, slipping seamlessly into lecture mode. 'It is an established scientific fact that as animal faeces breaks down it generates heat. Though above ground and in the top of the soil it is below freezing point, not far below the surface the slurry remains warm and soft, giving me as comfortable a landing as I could have hoped for. It is hardly a miracle, Sergeant Major, merely science in action.'

'I meant that of all the places to fall off the tank you happened to fall in the one soft bit of ground for miles around. That's the miracle.'

'Hmph.'

'Just think,' said the sergeant major, 'if Old Aggie hadn't kept a substantial pool of livestock effluent beside the track to her house, or if you had flown off the tank at a slightly different moment, you might have broken your neck. I never thought I would say this about you, Professor, but I'm glad to see you're OK.'

'OK? If you call being covered in a liberal coating of animal faeces being OK, then yes, I suppose I have never been better. There will be bruising, of course, but no bones appear to have been broken. And there is no need for you to all gawp at me like that. This is not the first time that life has emerged from some warm little pond. Now, how am I ever going to get this muck off me?'

'We're a hundred yards from Old Aggie's house,' said Reverend Potter. 'I'm sure she'll be happy for you to clean yourself up.'

The four men left the tank where it was and began the final trudge to the rubble stone farmhouse, which was surrounded by outbuildings and snow-covered farming equipment. Smoke was coming from the chimney and with it, the promise of warmth. 'I wonder if the doctor will be here,' pondered the Reverend.

'A doctor?' put in the Professor, who still looked like a walking poo with eyes and mouth. 'I do hope so. It would do me the world of good to have the opportunity to converse with a highly educated atheist for the first time since I don't know when. All doctors are, of course, atheists. In order to become a medical professional one must study a good deal of science, and anybody who gains even a basic knowledge of science will at once realise that all the experiments point in the same direction: to the non-existence of God. This is why I visit hospitals at every opportunity – hotbeds of atheism, each and every one of them. Sometimes I merely sit in the foyer and watch the staff as they come and go: doctors and nurses, each one profoundly awake to the plain fact that they are no more and no less than a collection of trillions of cells, that all of life, everything that makes us what we are, comes from the atoms within. Usually I don a disguise on these visits, because those in the medical profession look up to me so very much that if they recognise me they find it impossible not to approach me and offer words of thanks for everything I have done for science and reason. When they find out who I am they applaud me, like this.'

As he illustrated the enthusiastic clapping of a medical professional, globules of slurry flew from his hands, and the others moved beyond their range as quickly as they could.

'I do not wish to distract them from their duties,' he continued, 'so to avoid their attentions I wear a large hat and a false beard. I, of course, would have made a splendid doctor. Along with my unparalleled grasp of science, I would have had an exemplary bedside manner. But', he sighed, 'evolutionary biology came along, and medicine's loss is wider humanity's gain.' Some of the slurry trickled into his mouth, but he seemed not to notice.

'I think the Professor was right,' said the sergeant major to the vicar. 'It wasn't a miracle, him being saved by that big puddle of shit. The miracle would have been if he'd never come back to the surface.'

36

Smee had been anticipating a wretched scene at Old Aggie's farm cottage, and first impressions were consistent with this. Paint was peeling from the frames of the small windows and the barn door had come off its hinges. Through the snow could be seen the outline of a tractor with too few wheels for it to be of any use.

The vicar explained that Old Aggie had instructed him to come in without knocking, and they all followed. Smee was relieved to see that on the inside the place wasn't the shambles it might have been. It was simple and neat, with exposed stone walls and black wooden beams. Above all, it was warm.

And there before them, not confined to her bed but wrapped in a dressing gown, smiling and welcoming them all, stood Old Aggie. Smee had been expecting to find a toothless Quentin Blake illustration, a pile of skin, bone and wild hair raging against the dying of the light; but instead here was a bright-eyed old lady. She was ancient and tiny and frail, but she greeted the men with great warmth. She clearly knew the vicar and the sergeant major well. They spent a while catching up, and then it came time to meet the strangers.

'This is Smee,' said the vicar. Smee was touched when

this autumn leaf of a woman gripped his hand and told him how welcome he was. 'And this,' continued the vicar, 'is … oh.' His nose had adjusted to the Professor's new smell; amid the activity he had quite forgotten that one of their party was wearing a thick coating of effluvium.

'You've fallen into the slurry pit, haven't you?' said Old Aggie.

'I have, somewhat,' said the Professor.

'Oh, I am sorry,' she said. 'If you ask me, it's a daft place to put it. I used to tell my husband, but would he listen? And he was forever falling into it himself on the way home from the pub. I lost count of the times he came in looking like that. You go into the bathroom and clean yourself up.'

Old Aggie showed the Professor to a room just off the kitchen. She started filling the bath for him. 'It'll take a few soaks,' she explained, 'and there's the shower. It's probably best to go back and forth from one to the other.'

As the Professor began to clean up, the others sat around the kitchen table. Mrs Potter had sent a fruit cake, which was sliced into as tea was poured. Encouraged by the sergeant major and the vicar, Old Aggie told Smee tales of past times. He learned that in the Second World War she had piloted planes for the Air Transport Auxiliary and that, after the war, her husband had run the farm while she had worked as a school teacher. The sergeant major had been among her pupils. 'He always had the voice for it,' she joked. The sergeant major smiled at her recollections.

Smee listened to tales of farm life that seemed to come from a distant past. He felt choked with emotion at Old Aggie's good humour and stoicism as she told him how she had never had the children she had longed for, and how she had coped since losing her husband seventeen years earlier. Smee dared to ask her about her name and she explained that she had come from a long line of Aggies, who for generations had added the word *Old* to their names on their seventieth birthday. 'I don't know which one started it, but it's been a bit of a tradition up here for centuries. I have plenty of nieces and nephews,' she sighed, 'but I am the last of the Old Aggies. I feel I've let the others down, because when I go …'

As they all fell silent, Smee understood why Old Aggie meant so much to all of them. He had only known her for as long as it had taken to drink two cups of tea and eat a slice of cake, but she meant a lot to him too.

37

As the sound of showering and scrubbing came from the room next door, the anecdotes, amusing and melancholy, continued to flow.

'I hope you don't mind me saying,' said Reverend Potter, 'but I can't help noticing that you're seeming rather well.'

'I know. I'm sorry about that. I called Mrs P. this morning, but she told me you'd already left. I'd been in a bad way for days, but I woke up late this morning feeling a lot better. I'm so sorry for having brought you all this way in such terrible weather.'

The vicar and the sergeant major told her that it had been no trouble, and that they were glad to see her.

'Yesterday, though, the strangest thing happened to me. I was turning hot and cold, and I could feel my time had come. Now don't laugh at me, but for a moment I thought I had died. You see, everything went dark, and it was as if I was passing through a long tunnel.'

From the other side of the bathroom door came a loud snigger. The bathing Professor was listening in. Old Aggie didn't seem to hear him, and continued her story.

'At the end of the tunnel there was light, and God was waiting to meet me.'

There was another snigger, louder this time. Whether Old Aggie heard it or not, she continued.

'It was all very strange,' she said. 'He wasn't how I expected him to be. I always imagined him to be an old man with a long white beard, but he didn't look anything like that.'

'How did he look, Old Aggie?' asked the sergeant major.

'I feel silly saying it, but … he looked like a goblin with a purple face.'

Smee waited for a howl of derisive laughter from the bathroom, but none came.

Old Aggie carried on. 'He told me I had come to see Him too soon. He said I must go back, because there was one more thing He needed me for.'

And as she said this, Old Aggie began to look tired.

'I do apologise,' she said, 'but I think all this excitement has quite worn me out.' She turned to the vicar. 'Would you mind seeing me to my room? Perhaps we could say a little prayer together?'

Smee waited for the Professor to come bursting through the door, mocking the old woman for having made such a request. But the silence from the bathroom remained.

'Would you like me to change into my vicar's outfit?' he asked.

'Oh no. There's no need to stand on ceremony.'

The Reverend accompanied Old Aggie up to her room.

Every step was an ordeal for her. When at last they got there, she lay on her bed and closed her eyes. Together they said the Lord's Prayer, and Old Aggie's voice was so halting that she seemed like a different person from the one who just minutes earlier had been holding court at her kitchen table. Reverend Potter heard somebody enter the house; Old Aggie had told him to expect her niece to arrive at any moment. He felt relieved that he would not be leaving her alone. He had attended plenty of people in their final hours, and he knew he would not be seeing her again.

'Goodbye, Old Aggie,' he said.

There was no reply.

38

After a brief and solemn talk to Old Aggie's niece on the landing, Reverend Potter returned to the kitchen to find the Professor scrubbed to a shocking pink shine and wearing nothing but a towel around his waist.

'I hardly think this is suitable attire in which to deliver a speech on a matter of the utmost gravity,' he was saying. 'And my slurry-soiled garments are fit only for the furnace.' He held up a transparent plastic bag full of fetid clothes. 'Solve this one for me, Smee.'

Smee was stuck. A shrill beep came from inside the bag: the Professor's phone had survived the ordeal and had picked up a signal. Somebody had sent him a text message.

'Get that for me, would you?' he said, handing Smee the putrid bundle.

Smee rolled up a sleeve and plunged his hand in to retrieve the device. After a considerable time spent rummaging and squelching, he pulled it out and looked at the message. 'You have a voucher code for cut-price pizzas this coming Wednesday,' he said.

'Excellent,' said the Professor, rubbing his bare belly. 'I love pizza almost as much as I love biscuits. Tell them how much I love biscuits, Smee.'

'The Professor loves biscuits very much.'

As Smee washed his filthy arm in Old Aggie's bath, the vicar came to the Professor's aid. 'I brought a full change of clothes with me,' he said. 'Clean and dry, too. As long as you don't get thrown into another slurry pit you'll at least have something to wear for your talk.'

As Smee came back into the room, Old Aggie's cuckoo clock popped twice out of its nest. 'We only have thirty minutes to reach Upper Bottom,' he cried. 'Reverend, where are these clothes?'

The vicar picked up the bag he had brought with him, and pulled out his spare set of clean clothes. 'Pop this lot on, Professor,' he said. 'It's not exactly the done thing to allow you to wear them, but these are exceptional circumstances and we can't have you going about naked in this weather, can we?'

The Professor and Smee stood speechless as Reverend Potter held up a full vicar's outfit. Cassock, dog collar, it was all there, even jet black socks and shiny shoes. The Professor looked down at the towel around his waist, and again at the clothes on offer. Then back to the towel, and again at the vicar's clothes. All the while the cuckoo clock was ticking.

39

There were not many people on the road between Old Aggie's house and Upper Bottom. A few dog walkers, though, and path shovellers, and those who were alerted by the unusual noise and peered curiously through their cottage windows, were treated to the unusual sight of a military tank making its way along the country lanes. On top of this tank stood, apparently, a vicar, and by his feet sat a man of indeterminate age who was anxiously checking his watch every few seconds.

'I haven't warmed to you,' the sergeant major had said to the Professor as they left Old Aggie's house. 'I haven't warmed to you one little bit, but as long as you keep quiet I'll let you ride inside the tank.'

The Professor had not kept quiet, apparently unable to stop himself from using his borrowed vestments as the springboard for a monologue about institutional child abuse, and the HAM movement's official stance on the moral differences between violent buggery and mild touching. Before the driver had even started the engine the Professor had informed the sergeant major, who hadn't said a word, that he was incapable of clear, logical thought, and had been duly banished once again to the roof, where an icy breeze whistled up his cassock.

They passed a sign that read WELCOME TO UPPER BOTTOM – THE HEART OF THE BOTTOMS, and soon found themselves the sole moving vehicle on a small main street dotted with pubs and shops. There were a few people milling around who, without exception, stopped and stared at the majestic and fearsome tank, and the two men on top.

The tank took a right turn by a barber's shop, then a left by a bus shelter, and stopped by a small door, over which was the sign UPPER BOTTOM VILLAGE HALL – REAR ENTRANCE. Smee checked his watch yet again. It was twenty-nine and a half minutes past two.

Leaving the Professor on the tank, Smee jumped down and darted into the building in search of Mrs Smith. He went through a corridor and into the kitchen, where a robust grey-haired woman in tweed was filling a tea urn. Seeing the newcomer, she smiled.

'Hello,' she said, her smile fixed and her lips barely moving, almost like a ventriloquist. 'And who have we here?'

'My name is Smee, and I wonder if you can help me find Mrs Smith?'

'Smee!' she cried. 'How lovely to meet you. *I'm* Mrs Smith.' They exchanged a firm handshake. 'I had completely given up on you making it. How ever did you get up those hills?'

'We managed to get hold of an all-terrain vehicle,' he said.

'Well, that's wonderful. We've been at it too, darting around in tractors and four-wheel drives all day long getting everyone here for our charity event. How super that you could join us. I must say,' she continued, 'you don't look anything like your voice. I was expecting somebody very different indeed. But not to worry – you're a very handsome young man, and that's what counts. You *are* young, aren't you? I hope you don't mind me saying, but it's rather hard to tell.'

'I'm thirty-nine.'

'That's very young indeed in my book. Now where is this Professor of yours?'

'He's running through his lines. I was wondering, how long would you like him to speak for? He was thinking an hour and a half would be about right, followed by an hour of questions.'

'Oh dear. I'm afraid that would be much too long. We already have a full programme for our charity event, and I'm afraid we can only fit him in for about five minutes.'

'I see. That is rather a brief slot.' Smee dreaded the thought of telling the Professor that he wasn't going to be able to give the full lecture he had been planning.

'You've gone pale, Smee. Tell you what, since you've come all this way, how about we give the Professor *seven* minutes, with an extra three for questions, so ten minutes in total?'

'That would be preferable, Mrs Smith.'

'Super. Now, the stage is through there.' She pointed. 'You gather the Professor and wait behind the curtain. I have to go now and get on with the event.' She looked at her watch. 'I shall introduce him at two forty precisely. Will that do?'

'Perfectly, Mrs Smith. And thank you for having us.'

'Not at all. You know, you really do look different from your voice,' she said.

41

The Professor and Smee stood on the stage, in the darkness behind the curtain. From the hall came a muffled chorus of women's voices, so many speaking at once that not a word could be made out.

'So I have just ten minutes?'

'I'm afraid so, Professor.'

'Ten minutes in which to unravel lifetime after lifetime of deception and delusion.'

The men stood in silence. Smee knew not to disturb the Professor while he was gearing himself up for a big speech.

'Smee,' said the Professor, in an unfamiliar tone. 'I am experiencing a feeling of discomfiture.'

'Discomfiture? But why, Professor? Do you think you might be concussed?'

'No, there is no concussion, but things have not been usual these last days. I arrived in this area expecting to shake it to its very core. But I feel as though *I* am the one who has been shaken.'

Smee was taken aback. 'I am sure that as soon as the curtain opens your assurance will return.'

'I wish I shared your confidence, Smee. But for the first time in my life, I feel anxious at the thought of addressing an audience. I wonder if it would be better for all concerned were I to forego my speech today.'

After everything he had been through to get the Professor to the stage, Smee couldn't bear the thought of turning back. It was time for a pep talk. 'Professor,' he said, 'I know you can go out there and change those women's lives. Do as you have done so many times before, and present them with the folly of their beliefs. It is what you do; it is who you are. They will be shocked, but in the long run they will thank you for it. And let us remember, this is just the first domino to fall.'

The pep talk appeared not to have made any impact. 'Certain things have happened, Smee. What was it that stopped me from killing that cat? Perhaps it was the small child. It seemed to tug at my heartstrings. I didn't even realise I *had* heartstrings, and me a world-renowned biologist. And that is not all. Today I stared death in the face, and I saw a rainbow bridge and heard the music from the Hovis advert. And then, Smee, that old woman, did you hear what she said? She said she had seen a goblin with a purple face.'

'There is probably a rational scientific explanation for all those things.'

'Yes, Smee. There probably is. *Probably*. But just how sure can we ever truly be? I believe that the time has come for a downgrade.'

'A downgrade?'

'Yes. Until now I have been six point nine out of seven

certain that there is no God. But after the events of recent days, I feel that I must alter this to six point eight out of seven. And do you know what this means?'

'Er … not really.'

'It means that the figure has fallen below the threshold. At six point nine out of seven I have been scientifically justified in mocking people who believe in God, in ridiculing them with contempt. But at six point eight out of seven, well … it would not be acceptable science for me to do so. And with that gone, what do I have left? Brand Dawkins is fatally compromised and my empire turns to dust.'

There was a shuffle from the front of the stage. Something was being moved into position. 'That will be my lectern,' he said. 'I have been in this business long enough to know a lectern when I hear one. And for the first time in my life this is a lectern behind which I do not wish to stand. Oh, I should be strong but I am weak. I should be marble, but I am clay. Smee, I cannot do it. I am not going on.'

42

'I suppose I shall have to look for other avenues of employment,' sighed the Professor. 'Perhaps I shall move to Totnes and open a shop selling magic crystals. I have always been rather dismissive of that kind of thing, but you never know; there might be something to it, after all.'

'Professor, your nerves must be shattered after such an eventful day. I am going to give you some advice. I know that this sounds rather corny, but I have tried it myself and found it to be extremely beneficial: when speaking in public, it helps to imagine every member of your audience naked. It really puts one at ease.'

'Naked, you say? I suppose I could try, but if this doesn't work, Smee, there will be no talk.' There was the sound of a microphone being tested. 'How long have we got?'

Smee checked his watch. 'Twenty seconds.'

The Professor mumbled to himself. 'Naked, naked, naked, naked.' He found where the curtains met and with a finger he parted them, just enough to see through. He turned white and looked at Smee. 'Dear God, Smee. Dear God – even though it is a six point eight out of seven scientific certainty that He does not exist. That method of yours – it works. I looked out there and it really did seem as if they were completely naked, every single one of them, right down to their how-do-you-dos. It stands as testament to the incredible scientific properties of the human brain; all those neurons and so forth. I shall give you credit, Smee. This has helped me no end. I am reminded of the power of science. You are right: it has been a long day and my mental faculties have been compromised. But no longer – downgrade, be damned.' He looked up to the ceiling. 'Science, forgive me for my moment of doubt.'

There was a wave of feedback, followed by Mrs Smith's voice, loud and clear over the speakers. The Professor peered through the gap in the curtains again. 'It's still working, Smee. It is as if I can see her bare bottom, dimpled and grey, just feet from where we stand.'

He let the curtain close and they stood together, listening as they waited.

'Ladies, if I may have your attention please. As you know, we have all been greatly looking forward to Mrs Wood's slideshow about the hedgehog that has been visiting her garden, but because of her husband's back we've had to postpone it until January at the earliest. Straight after Mrs Wood called me with the news that she wouldn't be able to make it, my phone rang again. It was as if my guardian angel was watching over me.'

Smee looked at the Professor, waiting for him to smirk or sneer, but his expression did not change.

Mrs Smith carried on. 'I spoke to a very nice gentleman by the name of Smee, who asked me if we had a slot open for his friend Professor Richard Dawkins. I booked him right away. As soon as I was off the phone I looked up the Professor on the Internet and found out that he is very famous indeed, and has even been on the television.'

There was a collective 'Ooooh' from the audience.

'So it really is very exciting to have him here. As you all know he was stuck in the snow the other day, but he has gone to great lengths to get here this afternoon, and we are extremely grateful for that. Smee has asked me to point out that despite his clothing, the Professor is not a real vicar. Apparently he is "the opposite of a vicar". I'm not quite sure what that means, but I dare say we are about to find out. So will you please welcome, to give us a very quick talk on the subject of ...' There was a pause, which was clearly down to her putting on reading glasses and looking at her notes; Smee took this as his cue to scuttle into the wings. '... "Science and the non-existence of God", will you please give a warm All Bottoms welcome to our special guest speaker, Professor Richard Dawkins.'

The room filled with applause and the curtains opened. The Professor was on stage.

43

The applause continued as the Professor, still not used to wearing a cassock, shuffled over to his lectern. He blinked a few times, cleared his throat, blinked a few more times, ran his finger along the inside of his dog collar, rubbed his eyes as if he still couldn't quite believe what he was seeing, blinked a bit more, then began his speech.

'Good afternoon, ladies of the All Bottoms Women's Institute. I only have a short time in which to address you, so it is imperative that you listen very closely to everything I have to say. Please raise your hand if you believe in God.'

Around three quarters of the women put their hands up.

'An overwhelming majority, just as I expected. Now listen to me. Once upon a time there was nothing. Or almost nothing, anyway. Now there are lots of things. And in the interim there has been something called evolution. Those are facts, and there is so much evidence for those facts that anybody who questions any aspect of them is an idiot. Now let me tell you this: science has …' The Professor appeared distracted. He continued to blink and rub his eyes, looking from one apparently naked woman to the next. 'If there is one thing that science has done ... No, let me put it another way.' He was visibly struggling to regain his composure, and fell back on his mantra. 'There is no God,' he cried, banging his lectern as he strove to establish an air of authority, but even he didn't seem convinced by his outburst. 'At least, there probably isn't one. I cannot say with absolute certainty. Let us not be too hasty. You see, there was a cat having kittens.'

As one, the audience went 'Aaaaahhhhhh'.

The Professor carried on. 'Yes, yes. Quite. But it was having difficulties. I was ready to put it out of its misery; to feed it, tail first, through a mangle.'

They gasped.

He put a hand to his forehead. 'But something deep within me made me do everything I could for this cat and, sure enough, I did not kill it. Instead I did what was necessary to ensure that it, and its kittens, were safe.'

They sighed with relief.

'I put my fingers up its whatnot and out they came, brand new and, though it is rather unscientific to say so, those kittens were adorable little things. For the English cats are the best in Europe and, though they cannot fly, they clamber most excellently. I had, of course, been hoping that at least one of them would have carried a random genetic mutation which had transformed it into another species entirely; alas it was not to be. But no matter. And what's more there was a child there, I believe it was called Emily, and it melted my heart.'

There was another 'Aaaaahhhhh'.

'And I spent the rest of the day being kind to people and helping them out, and it made me feel nice to be kind to them. I felt a sort of warm feeling in my tummy ...' He gazed about, and noticed for the first time that he was surrounded by a stage set. 'I appear to be in a castle of some sort. Tell me, have I died?'

'No, Professor,' they reassured him. 'You're still alive. The amateur dramatics are doing *Cinderella*.'

'I see. I nearly died earlier today, though. Twice. And I saw a rainbow bridge and heard the music from the Hovis advert. But, as you can see, I did not die. And then an old lady thought she saw a goblin with a purple face. Maybe she did. Who am I to say?'

As if somebody had flicked a switch, this confused, rambling old man vanished and the Professor was back, his thunder fully restored. 'I shall tell you who I am to say: I am the most highly regarded evolutionary biologist of his age, that is who. I am six point nine out of seven certain that there is no God. Not six point *eight* out of seven; six point *nine* out of seven. I am sure you realise that we scientists mark everything out of seven. It is our way. But yes, it is six point nine out of seven, and I am so highly decorated that to disagree with me is to disagree with science itself. And yet,' his voice softened once again, 'our atheist bus did only say that there was *probably* no God. Grayling, of course, complained about this; he maintains that it should be seven out of seven but if you ask me, that's just showing off. Perhaps, ladies, perhaps you are right. There cannot, surely, be an old man with a beard who lives in the sky, but maybe there is much that will always be beyond our ken. And, let's be honest, they are still digging for that elusive fossil of a giraffe with a medium-length neck. Maybe it is six point eight out of seven after all. I just don't know what to think any more. And', he sighed, 'I am not even sure I am unanimous in that.'

The Professor stood behind his lectern, hunched and blinking, and Mrs Smith realised his speech had come to an end. She joined him on the stage.

'What an interesting little talk,' she said. 'I'm sure we all now have a much better understanding of …' She adjusted her glasses and checked her notes. '"Science and the non-existence of God". So does anybody have a very quick question for the Professor?'

A hand went up. 'Professor, can I ask you about these?' The woman took each of her nipples between finger and thumb. 'I understand why we ladies have them, but how about men? How come they haven't evolved away?'

'You seem to be tweaking your …'

'My nipples, Professor.'

'Do you mean that they are on display? I thought I was merely imagining that I could see them.'

'Oh no, Professor. We are all entirely naked. Didn't Mrs Smith tell you?'

Mrs Smith turned bright red. 'I'm terribly sorry, Professor. What with one thing and another I completely forgot to mention it. This is the photo shoot for our annual nude calendar. It's our second biggest charity fundraiser these days, after cakes. We've got a lot of orders already and it's due at the printers, so we'd better get back to it. I must say, this is something I've been wondering about for years; I've asked my husband but he doesn't seem to know, even though he's got a pair. So why is it that men have nipples?'

'Chromosomes,' mumbled the Professor. 'It's all to do with chromosomes.'

'Fascinating. Now, before I forget,' she said, looking at her clipboard, 'Joan and Rosemary, you are up next. You're going to be August, so we're going with a seaside theme. Rosemary, you cover your essentials with a beach ball, and Joan, you can use a bucket and spade. Now, does anybody have one final very quick question for our visitor?'

Another hand went up. 'If evolution is true, and I'm not saying it isn't, then how come there aren't any hairy fish flapping about by the water's edge?'

The Professor closed his eyes and hung his head. There was a long silence. Without looking up he said, quietly, 'I'm afraid I cannot answer that with absolute certainty.'

'Thank you, Professor,' said Mrs Smith. 'It's been a lovely talk. Now let's all give our visitor a nice big clap.'

The members of the All Bottoms Women's Institute applauded the Professor and waited for him to leave the stage. But he did not leave the stage.

44

'I was joking,' he roared, his expression resolute once again. 'Of course it is six point nine out of seven, and I can explain all that hairy fish nonsense with absolute authority. In fact I can go one better than that. Ladies of the All Bottoms Women's Institute, I am about to perform an experiment that will have you standing outside the church this coming Sunday, jeering at the congregation as they file in and out. I had been waiting until my forthcoming lecture at the Royal Albert Hall to demonstrate this, but impatience has won the day. Smee, bring on my apparatus and a stool.'

Smee picked up the chemicals case, hurried on stage with it and opened it up. He was greeted with applause.

'There's no need to clap him; he's only my male secretary,' said the Professor, as Smee hurried back to the wings to get a stool, which he brought on stage to the sound of his own footsteps. 'Now, I am going to show you people, once and for all, that there is no God. Using chemicals alone, I, Professor Richard Dawkins, shall now create life before your very eyes.'

'It's not going to take long is it, Professor?' asked Mrs Smith. 'It's just we are rather pressed for time.'

'Mrs Smith, it will take just a few moments.'

'Even so, Joan and Rosemary, would you get on with having your picture taken? The rest of us can watch the Professor create life while we're waiting to be called.'

Smee looked on from the side of the stage as the Professor took out four plugged test tubes, each containing liquid. 'All of life is just chemicals,' he explained. 'And I have spent many years working out which specific chemicals are the ones from which life springs. At last I have the answer.' He picked up a beaker and placed it on the stool, then one by one he added the contents of the test tubes. He swilled them round and they came together to make a gloopy off-white liquid.

'As I speak, the chemicals are reacting with one another, and I can assure you that conscious life will emerge from this concoction just as life emerges from the atoms that make up a hen's egg.'

The women looked on in silence. The photographer could be heard in the corner of the room. 'Up a bit with the bucket, Joan,' she was saying. 'I can still see your bits.'

Nothing seemed to be happening in the beaker.

'I cannot say what form this life will take: a hummingbird, perhaps, or a guinea pig, or a tench. At any moment one of those creatures might spring forth. I, of course, hope to have created a new species entirely, the likes of which will never have been seen before. Dawkinsia, I suppose they will wish to call whatever emerges, a request to which I shall graciously accede: *Dawkinsia Magnifica*.'

Everybody continued to stare at the beaker.

'What *are* you doing with that beach ball, Rosemary?'

'Of course it may take some time for the chemicals to fully react and for life to appear. I shall leave it there and – you mark my words – a creature will emerge.'

Mrs Smith looked concerned. 'What should we feed it?'

'Biscuits.'

'Oh.'

'Thank you for your time, ladies,' said the Professor. Leaving the beaker on its stool in the centre of the stage, he walked off, to the sound of polite applause. And when the applause was over, the naked women stayed where they were, looking warily at the beaker on the stage and hoping that a tiger wasn't about to leap out. Or, worse, a spider.

45

The Professor walked into the wings and kept going in the direction of the kitchen. Smee knew he ought to follow, to congratulate him on a job well done and agree with him when he said that he had illustrated beyond doubt that there was no God. But he stayed where he was.

He was vaguely aware that the speech had not gone well, that the Professor had drifted in and out of coherence and vacillated wildly. He had been a little taken aback when he peered around the edge of the curtain to discover that the audience really was naked, but apart from that the drama on and off stage had not made a particular impression on him. Instead he had found himself in a daze, reliving the pep talk he had given, which had helped to ensure that the speech had gone ahead. He realised his heart had not been in it.

His motivation had been skewed. He had been driven by a selfish need to finish his task, to not find himself scuppered just moments from achieving the purpose of their expedition. Mixed with this had been his concern for a confused old man. The Professor had never seemed so frail and human as he had that day, and Smee had not wanted to see him walk away from his life's work.

He had hoped that giving one of his speeches would go some way towards reinvigorating him, but he had not felt any pressing need for the members of the All Bottoms Women's Institute to be told in no uncertain terms that science had proved that there was no God.

He hadn't undergone a sudden conversion. The Bible remained as baffling to him as it ever had, and he couldn't see how it was possible to live life according to its stew of horror stories, gentle morality tales and threats of eternal sadistic violence. But he could understand why people tried. He, too, had needed something to cling to.

Smee wasn't only disenchanted by the Professor's crusade; he was also starting to feel embarrassed to be associated with it. He knew there was a debate to be had, that there were wealthy and powerful religious maniacs spewing anti-scientific nonsense, but in trying to silence his critics, and even the casually curious, by hurling insults at them, and by fighting battles on all fronts at all times, and digging up the Nazis, all he was doing was dragging his end of the debate into the gutter.

A lot had changed in the hours since Catherine had joined his quiz team. It was as if he had woken from a long and troubled sleep. He was going to call her and, if she said she didn't want to meet up with him, he would be disappointed, even a little heartbroken, but he wouldn't be surprised and he would survive. Up until his final pint, when it had all gone wrong, she had shown him that he was not a hopeless case, that he had the potential to return to being a functional person, even a man again. All he had needed was a glimpse of hope to set him free.

He remembered the experiment. He looked over to the beaker, to see if life had emerged. There was no sign of it. Not yet, anyway.

46

The Professor sat on a folding plastic chair in the kitchen of the Upper Bottom village hall. Mrs Smith joined him, still completely bare apart from a pair of reading glasses on a chain around her neck. 'What a super little talk, Professor. I'm terribly sorry about the mix-up over the calendar. Still, you are a biologist and I see from Wikipedia that you've had three wives, so I'm sure it's nothing you haven't seen plenty of times before. Now, I shall get you your fee. Seven pounds twenty, wasn't it? I shall just dig though my handbag.'

'Three wives,' mumbled the Professor. 'That reminds me: I made a scientific agreement with a simple old woman. I must honour this, and call the most recent specimen.' He took his phone from his cassock pocket and dialled. 'Hello dear,' he said. 'I am very well, thank you. And how are you? Good, good.'

Mrs Smith had found the seven pounds twenty in her purse. 'Here you are, Professor,' she said.

The Professor took the money and returned to his telephone conversation. 'What's that, dear? Yes, that is correct; there is a woman here with me. A naked woman, as it goes. Have I seen Upper Bottom? I haven't just *seen* Upper Bottom, I'm *in* Upper Bottom.' He looked at the phone. 'Blast it. It's gone dead again. That does it. Smee must find me a new phone company. Smee,' he called.

Smee did not come running.

'I'm afraid I have a little confession to make, Professor,' said Mrs Smith. 'I have a daughter who's an atheist, just like you, and I've just sent her a text message boasting about how I've met you. She's a science teacher on the Isle of Wight – deputy head of department, as a matter of fact.'

'It is fortifying to be reminded that there are people out there with intelligence and common sense. Do pass on my warmest regards.'

Mrs Smith's phone hummed in her handbag, and she took it out. 'Oh look, she's written straight back. I shall read it out: "Tell him from me that he's a great big bell-end." I'm not sure what a bell-end is, but I have a feeling it's a terrific compliment.' The Professor said nothing, and she carried on. '"He's an embarrassment to atheism, and I can't think of anyone who works harder to put people off science." Isn't that n—… Oh, hang on, that *wasn't* especially nice, was it? I shall have words with that young lady about her manners. I'm terribly sorry, Professor, but I was under the impression that all atheists and scientists thought you were smashing. Still, I always say that you can't please all of the people all of the time. Isn't that right, Professor?'

The Professor said nothing.

'Professor?'

He stared straight ahead.

47

Some time after the Professor's call, Smee supposed he had better find him. His only aim now was to get him into the tank and back to Market Horten. He would wait until he had achieved that before making any decisions about what to do next. He knew, though, that his tenure as a male secretary was coming to an end. He found him in the kitchen, sitting alone.

'Let's get going, Professor,' he said.

The Professor nodded, but before he had a chance to stand up, the door opened and Mrs Smith came back in, accompanied by another of the women. Both were still completely unclothed. 'Ah, the Professor and Smee. I'm so glad we caught you before you left. We have a little something for you to take away. Beryl here has baked you a lovely cake, haven't you, Beryl?'

Beryl nodded.

'It's her own recipe, too. It's the first time she's ever tried it, and she's given it a special name.'

'It's called Professor cake,' said Beryl.

'How about that, Professor?' said Mrs Smith. 'Having a cake named in your honour? And I'm sure it'll be like no cake you have ever tasted before. Beryl has won prizes, you know. She came first in the regional cake-baking open tournament, in the winter vegetables category. Although she *was* the only entry in that section, weren't you, Beryl?'

'Nobody else seems interested in putting winter vegetables in cakes, Professor, which is a shame because it does give them quite an interesting flavour. I've mainly used sprouts for yours, but you may notice a little hint of parsnip.'

'Oh,' said the Professor, still looking glazed.

'And the best thing is that sprouts and parsnips contain so much natural sweetness that I've not even had to add any sugar.'

'It sounds delicious,' said Smee.

'Now you go and get it, Beryl,' said Mrs Smith.

Beryl went away and moments later she was back, holding a huge rectangular cake. 'I've decorated it specially for you.' She placed it on the Professor's lap.

'I am quite lost for words,' he said.

'As am I,' said Smee. In neither case was this a figure of speech. They had no idea how to react to having two naked women present them with a sprout-based cake upon which had been iced a picture, in almost lifelike detail, of the Professor sitting in a wheelchair and being pushed along by a smiling Desmond Tutu.

'There were one or two mix-ups along the way,' said Mrs Smith, 'but I'm sure you won't mind.'

'I'm afraid I thought you were the other one,' Beryl explained to the Professor. 'I had already done the wheelchair, but luckily I found out my mistake before I got to the face. Let's just pretend you have a terrible ingrowing toenail.'

'Or that you're recovering from having had a kneecap replaced,' put in Mrs Smith. 'That happened to one of our ladies, and she was in a wheelchair for quite a few weeks. It was terribly uncomfortable for her, but it was lovely to get some use out of our special ramp. Those nice men went to all that trouble to put it in, and it was super to see it in active service at last. I always made sure she had extra cups of tea so our special loo would get some use as well. And I'm afraid *I* made a little booboo, too,' she confessed, pointing at the cake. 'I thought from his voice that Smee was a coloured gentleman. You do sound rather coloured on the phone, Smee.'

'Oh. Do I? Nobody's ever said that before.'

'That's supposed to be you, you see, pushing the wheelchair. You don't mind, do you? You look a little taken aback. I hope you're not offended.'

'No,' said Smee. Mrs Smith and Beryl were looking at him, hoping for reassurance, and he supposed he should say something else to underline his lack of concern. 'Black people do often have very pleasant voices, so I shall take it as a compliment.'

'They do sound nice, don't they?' said Mrs Smith. 'I suppose that's why so many of them become singers. I'm relieved that you're not upset. It would have been a little embarrassing for Beryl if you had been a racist.'

'Since I didn't know what you looked like,' said Beryl, 'I just iced a picture of my favourite coloured gentleman, Desmond Tutu. I have a bit of a soft spot for him, I must confess,' she said, blushing.

'I think we *all* have a soft spot for Archbishop Tutu,' said Mrs Smith.

'And before I forget,' said Beryl, 'don't eat the archbishop's robe all at once. The purple colouring might make you hyperactive, so just have a little at a time.'

'Duly noted, Beryl,' said Smee. 'Thank you.'

The Professor continued to stare at the cake.

'Now, Professor,' said Mrs Smith. 'I just checked on *Dawkinsia Magnifica*, and there's no sign of life yet. I wonder, would you let me into your secret? What are the ingredients?'

'I would be insane to reveal that before I have published my findings in a reputable journal. I am currently in deep negotiations with the *Mail on Sunday*.'

'Well, I wish you all the best with that. But when should we give up on it and pour it down the sink?'

'Pour it down the sink? That would be like picking all the apples from Newton's orchard before one has a chance to fall on his head. Life will emerge, Mrs Smith, you mark my words; and when it does, your belief in God will collapse like a house of cards.'

'Not at all, Professor. After all, God made the atoms, didn't He?'

The Professor sighed. 'That is a transparently feeble

argument,' he said. 'Weak as water. Smee, I do not have the energy. Mock her on my behalf, would you? Ridicule her with contempt.'

Smee looked at Mrs Smith, then at the Professor. Everything was clear, and he knew what he had to do. It felt like jumping down a well, but his descent was serene and he had a good feeling that there would, eventually, be a soft landing. 'No, Professor,' he said. 'She just has a different way of looking at things and we should treat that with respect, not contempt. After all, nobody knows everything.'

The Professor pointed a finger at Smee. 'You would defy me,' he hissed. 'Apostate! Creationist!' Then came the words he had once feared, but which no longer held the slightest power: 'You have ceased to be my male secretary.'

The door burst open and a world-weary looking middle-aged man with a drinker's nose strode in. 'Police,' he said, holding up his ID card.

48

'Hello Brian,' said Beryl, waving.

'Hello Beryl,' said the detective. 'Hello Mrs Smith. Oh,' he said, noticing at last that the women were entirely nude. 'I do apologise, ladies. I had no idea …' He looked at his shoes.

'Not at all, Brian – I mean, *officer*,' said Mrs Smith, taking command of the situation. 'We're busy posing for our annual charity calendar. Would you rather we covered up? It's just we are a little pressed for time, and we could be called over by the photographer at any moment.'

'No, I mustn't obstruct the progress of your calendar. I've already got my order in, as ever. But if you've got a moment …' He handed Mrs Smith a photograph. 'Have you seen anybody who resembles this gentleman? We have reason to believe he is in the vicinity.'

'Now,' said Mrs Smith, putting on her reading glasses and giving the photograph a long look. 'Well, well. He looks a lot like our friend here, the one with the enormous cake on his lap.'

'That vicar?' said the policeman. 'Well, I suppose there is a similarity.'

The Professor craned his neck to see the picture. 'It

looks nothing like me. Tell them, Smee.'

Smee could see that the resemblance was startling, but in spite of his recent dismissal, his instinct was still to protect the old man. 'Chalk and cheese,' he said, but he knew his tone was half-hearted.

The policeman walked over to the Professor, put the photograph beside his face and looked from one to the other. 'There is a bit of a likeness,' he said. 'But the man we're looking for is the opposite of a vicar. You see, we're on the hunt for somebody who is believed to be impersonating …' He pointed to the photograph. 'A famous scientist by the name of Richard Dawkins.'

49

'An impersonator?' spluttered the Professor. 'Why, he must be caught straight away. I will not be impersonated. Don't just stand there. Off you go and apprehend the scoundrel.'

'So *you* are Richard Dawkins?'

'Of course I am Richard Dawkins. Who do you think I am?' He pointed at his hair. 'A. C. Grayling?'

'You are the *real* Richard Dawkins?'

'Of course I am real. Now be off with you.'

'There's no need to be upset, sir. I'm just rather surprised to bump into you here because, when we spoke on the telephone earlier today, you told me you were in Chicago, promoting your autobiography. Do you remember?'

'I remember no such thing. I suggest you get the next plane to that Chicago place and arrest the *real* impostor.'

'Yes, I shall do that,' he said. 'I shall do that right now. I'll see what I can do about arranging a flight.' He reached into his pocket, as if to take out a phone. But when his hand emerged it was holding not a phone but a whistle. He put it to his lips and blew. Moments later, two uniformed officers came in.

The Professor took one look at the newcomers and,

clutching the cake, sprang to his feet and ran out of the room in the direction of the stage. He made straight for the break in the curtain and, watched by many startled naked women, he bounded down into the hall and sprinted for the exit. But when he was no more than halfway across the room, he became entangled in his cassock and fell, landing face first in the Professor cake. He got straight back to his feet, but by then it was too late. The police had surrounded him, and from the main entrance came a team of paramedics.

Smee stood on the stage and watched the drama unfold. The Professor was hunched over, his face contorted and smeared with the icing from the archbishop's robe. He was struggling desperately to get away. 'Welby must be behind this,' he spluttered. His voice was raspy; some of the cake must have lodged in his throat. 'Smee, go on to that Internet thing and tell them it is all to do with Welby. He is running scared and would silence me. Or perhaps Grayling. Yes, that must be it: Grayling is trying to seize my crown. You are henceforth reinstated. You get to the bottom of this, Smee.'

But Smee did not move. He looked on as the Professor was restrained and very deftly put into a straitjacket. 'Come along, now,' said one of the paramedics. 'Let's get you to the hospital.'

'To the laboratory, you say?' said the Professor, now absolutely calm. 'Yes, yes. Of course. I have wasted too much of my time here. I must go to the laboratory, to resume my experiments. Take me to the laboratory would you, my good men and, indeed, women? Let us not forget the ladies.'

The policemen and the members of the Upper Bottom Women's Institute stood in a sympathetic silence as the Professor allowed himself to be led away.

Smee remained on the stage, not sure what to do. With the episode over, the women got back to their photo shoot. A couple of them came out with a mop and bucket to clear away the splatters of Professor cake and, with the mess gone, their afternoon seemed to continue as if nothing unusual had happened.

A pair of young policemen wandered around the place. One of them carefully put the beaker into an evidence bag.

Smee walked over to the rear entrance, where the sergeant major and the vicar were waiting for him. They greeted him without a word. Smee knew they were being kind to do so, and he accepted their pity. He had certainly earned it.

As he climbed up on to the tank, an air ambulance passed overhead. At last the Professor had his helicopter.

50

Reverend Potter, Smee and Dave had the Wheatsheaf to themselves. Smee was glad to have company as he did his best not to die of embarrassment while he pieced things together.

He knew he should have realised from the start that the real Richard Dawkins would hardly be inclined to find personal assistants on Internet forums, or to spend weeks on end traipsing around the backwaters of Britain on trains and buses, giving talks in village halls and standing on upturned crates in shopping centres. And even if he *had* decided to travel around this way, he wouldn't have expected his assistant to pay for everything, never once putting his hand in his own pocket. Smee had taken the thick wad of receipts he had been keeping and thrown it on to the Potters' fire; he knew there was no hope of being reimbursed for all the meals and accommodation bills and travel costs. He had lost thousands of pounds, and was nearing the end of his redundancy money.

Above all, he supposed that the real Richard Dawkins would be unlikely to go around showing people Polaroids of a cataclysmic poo he had done after eating much too much chocolate. No alarm bells had rung, though, and he had retained an absolute belief in the impostor, right up until the moment he had darted away from the police and fallen, face first, into an enormous cake.

The others were quick to reassure him that his mistake had been understandable. They told him that the fake Richard Dawkins looked authentic enough, and the force with which he expressed his opinions had seemed consistent with the public image projected by the real one. Dave and the Reverend took turns to tell Smee about times they had made mistakes which, with hindsight, seemed entirely avoidable. With each new tale of misfortune, Smee felt a little better.

Having finished writing up the day's events, the detective joined them. He stayed on neutral topics, mainly catching up on local gossip with Dave and the vicar. He drank fast, though, and after about half an hour, when he was nearing the end of his fifth pint of lager, the pub had filled up a little and a hum of conversation allowed them to talk without being overheard.

'Brian,' said Reverend Potter, 'isn't it time you became wonderfully indiscreet?'

'If I must,' he sighed. He leaned into the group and started telling them what he knew of the background to the story. He had been put on the case the day before, and his briefing was fresh in his mind.

Smee listened intently. 'So you're saying he was an escaped mental patient?'

'No, no,' said Brian. 'Absolutely not. Nothing of the

sort. Let's nip that in the bud. He was a ... Let me think ...' He closed his eyes as he tried to recall the words. 'He was a "self-liberated personage of special psychiatric interest". That's what we have to call them these days. It's political correctness gone mad, if you ask me, but strictly between us, yes, he was an escaped mental patient. He got out by hiding in a big wicker laundry basket about three and a half weeks ago.'

'So how did he end up in hospital in the first place?'

'It all started earlier this year. He's a professor of business studies at a university somewhere or other.'

Smee knew it didn't make sense, but he found himself relieved to hear that he had been a real professor.

'He had gone through a divorce and was a little hard up, so to make a bit of money he signed up with a lookalikes agency and started taking on work as a Richard Dawkins impersonator at conferences and cocktail parties. He would mingle with the guests and people would have their picture taken with him, and he would get up and give a little speech, ranting and raving about how God doesn't exist, and how we're all part turnip, and how anybody who disagreed with him was an idiot. It was supposed to be a bit of fun, but he was very professional and did all the research and he would always stay in character for the whole event.'

Smee recalled how he had hung on the Professor's every word. 'And I thought he was a genius,' he said.

'He *is* a genius,' said Brian. 'It's just he's a genius when it comes to business studies.'

Smee couldn't work out whether this made him feel better or worse.

The detective carried on. 'Apparently the problems started when he was booked to appear at a launch party for an alternative comedian who had a DVD of amusing songs coming out. His management knew how much he loved Dawkins, so they booked the lookalike. The trouble was, the comedian thought he was the real thing and made a bee-line for him. He kept shaking his hand and saying, "Streuth, the best scientist ever, at *my* launch party. This is the most humble day of my life." Nobody had the heart to tell him and he spent the rest of the evening listening to the lookalike, agreeing with him like a nodding dog and saying, "Can I put that in a poem?" By the end of the evening the impersonator was so far into character that he couldn't come back out. The doctors think he had felt so loved by the alternative comedian that he couldn't bear to return to life as a lonely divorcee.'

Smee knew how the mind could tangle as it struggled to make things seem better. For weeks he had been happy to live a lie, being somebody he was not. He was glad he had snapped out of it though. He told himself he wasn't Smee any more; he was back to being Michael, and he needed to sort his life out as Michael, not as anybody else.

Brian carried on. 'He was reported missing by his work and was found a fortnight later in a green room at the

BBC, getting ready to be interviewed by Jeremy Vine. If it's any consolation, he wasn't tricking you: he absolutely believed that he was the real thing. I remember the good old days, when people like him used to think they were Napoleon, or Cleopatra, or Henry VIII, but now they all think they're Richard Dawkins, or Lynne Truss, or Danny Alexander. There are hospitals overflowing with them.'

'So that wasn't the real Lynne Truss he used to write to?'

'No, but try telling *him* that.'

'And what about all those phone calls to his wife?'

'The records show he only ever called the speaking clock. It was all going on in his head.'

'It's a bit sad really, isn't it?' said Dave. 'I know he didn't write them, but I'm still quite glad I didn't tell him I'd never made it past chapter three of any of his books. It might have hurt his feelings.'

Not for the first time, Michael chose not to mention that of all Richard Dawkins' books he had only ever read *The God Delusion*, and even then he had skimmed over the more academic passages. He had been happy just to know that he was backed up by a great intellect when making his contributions to Internet discussions, that a highly regarded scientist had apparently provided hard evidence that fitted in with his existing disbelief in all things supernatural. On his travels he had tried to fill the gaps in his knowledge, looking up the Professor's sound bites on the Internet while he napped. He had seen no great difference between the quotes he found online and the words that came from his companion's mouth. For all his catching up, Michael's grasp of the real Richard Dawkins' scientific work remained sketchy. He still had no idea what a *normal* phenotype was, let alone an extended one.

The detective finished his pint, wiped his mouth on his sleeve and said, 'Remember – you heard none of that from me.'

It was Michael's round, and when he went to the bar he found the courage to ask the barman about the woman in black.

She had left that afternoon, as soon as the roads had cleared. Warm air had moved in, and the thaw had begun.

Tuesday, 24th December

51

Michael Cartwright had been hard at work all day behind the bar of the Wheatsheaf and, after a quick shower and a change back at the Potters' house, he was getting ready to go back there for a night out. He had been invited to stay in the gnome-filled room until bookings picked up in the spring. They hadn't asked for any money but he had insisted on paying his way and, with perfect timing, a few shifts at the pub had opened up.

There had been nothing much to collect from his flat, but the day after the talk to the WI he had returned there, emptied it out and handed back the keys. He had taken the opportunity to call his estranged wife and arrange to meet her for a coffee to discuss the implications of their forthcoming house sale and decree absolute. She had been surprised to see him looking so well and being so happy, and he had been relieved to find that he could hold a civilised conversation with her. He even found himself on good form, and several times he made her nose wrinkle up with laughter in the way that had driven him crazy when they had first met. He told her he was moving away, that he was going to be lodging with a retired vicar and his wife in a town she had never heard of.

'So you've got religion? That's a turnaround.'

'No,' he laughed. 'I've not got religion, but I need a fresh start and they're nice people. I really like them.' Desperate for time away from the religion-versus-science tussle, he changed the subject. Without having planned it, and without so much as a prickle of pain, he found himself asking, 'How's Laurence?'

'I've not seen him for a while.'

'So he's disappeared in a puff of smoke?'

She nodded. 'Michael, you know this divorce business?'

'Er ... yes.'

'You don't think we're rushing into it, do you?'

Michael looked at his wife. She had hardly changed since the day they met. Any resentment he had harboured since she left had melted away, and he found he could even like her again. He pictured the phone number folded in the darkness of his wallet. 'No,' he said. 'Let's just get it over with.'

She nodded. 'You're right. Let's.'

52

Dave had handed his taxi over to his brother-in-law and joined Michael at the bar of the Wheatsheaf, which was busy with Christmas Eve revellers.

'Did that girl ever call back?' asked Dave.

Michael nodded.

'You don't seem too happy about it.'

'She wanted to see me again.'

'So what's the problem?'

'She said she wanted to do a project on me for her psychology course, about how heartbroken men go a bit loopy on the Internet. She wants to find ways we can be helped.' He had told Dave about his dark days and how they now seemed to have happened to somebody else, a desperately unhappy creature that had been trapped inside him. 'She thinks of me as a case study.'

Dave had reassured him that everybody has funny turns from time to time. 'It's a start, anyway. She'll see you're better now, forget her project and go out with you properly. Look at Sigmund Freud. That's how he met his wife: she came to him as a patient, and bingo.'

'Really?'

'Well, probably not. I just made that up, but don't give up hope. All you have to do is tell her you don't want to be her patient, but you do want to take her to the pictures.'

'Good advice, Dave. I'll do that. And if she says no, at least I'll know I'm capable of moving on.'

'That's it, Mikey boy,' said Dave. 'You're moving on like a good 'un. If I was to give you a mark out of ten for putting the past behind you and not letting it drag you down, I would give you a ten.'

Dave held his glass up to drink to Michael's fresh start. Michael happily clinked glasses with his new friend and, as he did, he caught something out of the corner of his eye. A newcomer had walked in, and he could feel a stare drilling into him. He turned his head to see who it was. His mouth flopped open.

Dave followed Michael's gaze. 'It's him, isn't it? The real one.'

Michael closed his mouth and nodded.

The newcomer's face broke into a smile, and he walked towards the men. 'I come in peace,' he said. 'It's Michael, isn't it? And you must be Dave. I've heard rather a lot about you two gentlemen.' Hands were pumped, and Dave brought the newcomer into the round with a pint of beer.

Their visitor spotted the dartboard. 'Who's for a game of arrows?' he asked.

Michael and Dave were glad of the opportunity to break the ice with a bit of old-fashioned male bonding.

'Sounds like a plan to me, Prof,' said Dave.

He held up a hand. 'Please, Dave. I have left the professoring behind.'

'Then what should we call you? Mr Dawkins? Richard? Richie? Rick? Ricardo? Rickadoodledoo? Tricky Dickie D.?'

He scratched his chin for a moment, and said, 'I currently hold thirteen doctorates so the proper way to address me is "Doctor Doctor Doctor Doctor Doctor Doctor Doctor Doctor Doctor Doctor Doctor Doctor Doctor Dawkins", but as this is an informal setting I shall permit you to call me simply "Doctor Doctor Dawkins".' He stopped himself. 'But no ... in honour of the occasion, I feel a humble "Doctor" will suffice.'

'Sounds good to me, Doc,' said Dave. 'Let's step up to the oche.'

They agreed to play a three-hander. Dave and Michael acquitted themselves well enough, but the Doctor was sensational. He finished in eleven darts, capping his victory with a nonchalant throw to the absolute centre of the bullseye.

'How do you do it?' asked Dave, as they sat at a table.

'It's basic science – combined, of course, with extensive practice. To let you into a secret, I have been thinking about going professional. My dear friend the late world champion Jocky Wilson assured me I would be able to compete at a high level and that, without book writing and lecturing taking up so much of my time, I might even reach the pinnacle of the sport. I used to make secret visits to his flat in Kirkcaldy, where he coached me to breaking point and beyond. He would sit there on the sofa shouting at me until I got it right. Jocky was sure that darts would be a way forward for me. He and I were planning some exhibition matches together before he passed away. We were going to be billed as "the Doc and the Jock", and we even had tentative bookings at the Lakeside Country Club and the Oxford Union when, tragically, the curtain fell.' The Doctor looked close to tears. 'I wonder, might we have a minute's silence for the great man?'

Dave and Michael were only too happy to accommodate this request. They looked grave and said nothing as the hubbub continued around them. The Doctor followed the second hand on his watch. 'One minute barely seems enough for a character such as Jocky. Let us remember him for one minute more.' That happened again, and again, and it wasn't until the end of the seventh minute of silence that he took his eyes from his watch. 'To Jocky,' he said, raising his glass.

Dave and Michael joined in. 'To Jocky.'

'Now, I believe the convention is for me to stand my round. Who's for a refill?'

They had time for one more before midnight mass began, and the Doctor went off to get the drinks.

'He doesn't seem so bad,' said Dave. 'He's better than the last one, anyway.'

Michael nodded, still rattled by being so close to the

real thing. He was relieved, though, that this one seemed to have more range to his conversation.

The Doctor returned, carrying three pints without spilling a drop. 'Let me check my change,' he said. He put a small pile of coins and a ten-pound note on the table. He held the note up to the light. This received his approval and he moved on to the coins, biting each one. 'It is possible to spot a fake this way,' he explained. 'It's basic science.' When he had bitten every coin, he declared that his change seemed to be genuine. 'Now let me check yours, Michael. Empty your wallet.'

Michael took out his wallet and placed all his money on the table. The Doctor held the notes up to the light and one by one bit all the coins. 'Every one the real deal,' he concluded. 'Dave, it's your turn.'

Dave had raided his tip jar and had quite a pocket full of change. The Doctor went through every coin, even down to the coppers, verifying their authenticity.

'Not a dud among them,' he said, pushing the pile back across the table to Dave. 'I have arranged lodgings at this very hostelry, so later on I shall offer to check the landlord's entire float. What an evening this is turning out to be. I have been able to indulge my three favourite pastimes: drinking, darts and checking for forged currency. Nowadays, with all my writing and lecturing, I can barely find the time to indulge my hobbies. And here's a little nugget of trivia for you: I have been diligently checking currency for over twelve years, and I have not once found a fake banknote or coin. It just goes to show, doesn't it?'

Michael and Dave nodded, neither of them quite able to work out what it went to show. Before they had a chance to ask, the church bells began to ring, heralding the start of the service. They drank up and got ready to go.

'You coming, Doc?' asked Dave.

53

The service had been a great success. The church was packed, and Reverend Potter's sermon had struck the perfect balance of festivity and solemnity. The Doctor had participated with great enthusiasm, his voice ringing out through the church, adding a rich layer to the festive sound of the carols. His command of 'Away in a Manger' even drew admiring glances.

When it was over they headed back through the churchyard and across the green towards the Wheatsheaf, where a nightcap awaited them, along with a few other discreetly invited friends of the landlord. A wind had picked up and there were a few spots of rain.

'So,' said Michael, to the Doctor. 'Did you just happen to be in the area?'

'I finished the promotional tour for my autobiography this afternoon and decided to make a small detour on my way home. I'd read a few articles about that impostor business and thought it would be a bit of fun to track down the participants.'

Michael had been following the articles too, and had even been interviewed and photographed for some of them. It hadn't been until he had read one of them that he had found out the Professor's recipe for life:

the police laboratory had identified milk of magnesia, lemon cordial, a few drops of Henderson's relish and a dash of human urine. Michael had not told anybody, but he had a feeling the urine had been his. The Professor had asked him for samples from time to time and he hadn't thought twice about handing them over. Had it come to life, *Dawkinsia Magnifica* would have been his child.

One reporter had visited the impostor in hospital, but hadn't come away with much more than the patient's thoughts on the atheist philosophies underlying *Deal or No Deal*. They had reported, though, that he seemed content, and remained resolute in his belief that he was the real Richard Dawkins and that there was either a six point eight or six point nine out of seven certainty that there was no God.

'I shall be off home in the morning for roast goose and sprouts with my third wife,' the Doctor continued, as they made their way across the green. The rain was getting heavier all the time and clouds had covered the moon. 'She used to be in *Doctor Who*, you know. But what a curious business that impersonator episode was. I suppose that when one attains the extraordinary level of fame that I have, such instances are bound to arise from time to time. My suspicions were raised when my legal team alerted me to news stories about me being kind to cats and reassuring people about their goldfish. They knew as well as I that I would never be kind to a cat or reassure anybody about their goldfish; there would be no point. It's not exactly a boon for the old reputation to be portrayed as some kind of sentimental buffoon.'

They had reached the middle of the green. 'Thank God it's all over, eh, Doc?' said Dave.

The Doctor stopped dead. 'I beg your pardon ... what did you just say?'

'Er ... Thank God it's all over, I think.'

'Thank what?'

'*God*.'

The Doctor threw his head back and howled with laughter. 'Oh, this is priceless!' he cried. '*Thank God*, indeed. You do realise, don't you, that there is no God? No God at all. Oh, just wait until I tell my dear friend the children's author Philip Pullman.' He pulled an iPhone from his pocket. 'I'm rather a whizz with this thing, you know; I often use it to tweet handy facts about Muslims.' He tapped away at the screen for a while. 'There. Do you wish to see?'

He showed them the screen and through the raindrops they read the sent message: 'Pullers, it's Dickie. Have been in conversation with man who said "Thank God".'

'Pullman spends most of his waking hours staring at a blank screen, waiting for me to get in touch. I dare say a reply will be imminent. Ah, here he is.' He looked at the screen and laughed. 'Read this.'

Again, Michael and Dave looked at the wet screen: 'ROFL!!!!!! He might as well have thanked the woodcutter from *Little Red Riding Hood*!!!!! It's all fairy stories!!!!!!!!!!!!!!!!!!'

'Excellent use of exclamation marks there,' said the Doctor. 'But then you would expect that from such a highly acclaimed author. He used to be a school teacher, you know.'

'Never mind all that, Doc,' said Dave. 'We're getting wet here. Let's get to the pub.'

The Doctor seemed not to hear him. 'There is no God, can you not see? I have done all the experiments and I am telling you, there is no God.'

Michael felt an awful sense of déjà vu, which was only heightened when the Doctor pointed a finger at him.

'Just ask Smee,' he said. 'Ask Smee if there is a God. Go on, Smee,' he said. 'Tell him. Tell this *Dave* character whether or not God exists.'

Michael looked at the Doctor, and then at Dave. '*I* don't think so, Dave,' he said, 'but you never know. Maybe He does, maybe He doesn't. It's not for me to say.'

The Doctor let out a roar of mirthless laughter. 'Maybe the moon is made of cheese, or maybe it isn't. It is not for you to say, is it, Smee?'

'Come on you two,' said Dave. 'Let's not worry about that kind of thing now. Let's get in the dry and have a drink.' The rain was coming down harder and harder.

Dave began to walk towards the light of the pub, and Michael followed. The Doctor stayed where he was, glassy-eyed and cackling. After a few paces, Michael turned around. 'You know where to find us,' he said. 'Don't be out here too long.'

He and Dave carried on to the Wheatsheaf, leaving their visitor in the middle of the green. The wind carried the occasional burst of his voice in their direction. 'Fairies at the bottom … evidence … the fossil record … I am unanimous …'

There was a flash of light, followed a few seconds later by a clap of thunder.

'I'm not sure he should be in the middle of the green in an electrical storm,' said Michael.

'He'll be fine,' said Dave. 'He's a scientist; he'll be wearing the right kind of shoes. Let's just leave him to it. He'll come in when he's good and ready.'

54

Michael and Dave were standing at the bar drinking a festive whisky when the pub's door opened. They expected to see a drenched Doctor, but in walked a drenched Brian the detective. 'You haven't seen another of those Richard Dawkins impersonators, have you?' he sighed.

Michael wilted.

'Poor bloke,' said Dave. 'No wonder he's a bit funny; it's enough to drive anyone potty. We haven't seen an impersonator,' he explained, 'but we've got the real thing, if that helps. He's out on the green right now, shouting at the sky.'

'The real one?' Brian took out a notebook and pencil. 'Apart from this shouting at the sky, has he been acting strangely at all?'

'No, not really. He made us have a seven-minute silence for Jocky Wilson, and then he started biting money, but that's normal for people like him, isn't it? They're all a bit weird.'

'Dave,' said Michael, 'maybe ...'

'Oh,' said Dave, the penny dropping. 'Yes, maybe. You could be right. Well, hit me with a ... Oh, never mind.'

'Darts and biting money?' said Brian, tapping his

notebook. 'He does sound authentic, but they're getting cannier and cannier. The one we're looking for has even had plastic surgery. He escaped from his hospital a few days ago, disguised as Father Christmas, and there have been a few reported sightings not too far from here. But you never know, maybe the real one is in the area. Let's go and have a chat with this new friend of yours.'

They went back out, into the wind and rain.

55

The clouds were thick, and council cuts had seen to it that the street lights had switched off at midnight, but through the dark a furious voice carried on the wind: 'It is piffle ... I have done the experiments ... a yellow and blue toothpaste monster ...'

They followed the raging as best they could. And then there he was, lit up at the sharp end of a bolt of lightning. He was thrown to the ground. They walked towards him and, as they neared, he got to his feet. His hair was standing on end and his clothes had been burned off.

'Fascinating,' he bellowed, seeming not to notice the others. 'Science struck me down, and science saved me. Had it not been for my footwear I would have perished, and at no point did I pray for salvation.' They could see his feet through the gloom. One of them was bare: a shoe had been torn off by the extraordinary force of the strike. The remaining shoe and its corresponding sock were the only items of clothing he still had on.

'Come, thunderbolts,' he cried, 'and singe my grey head once again.' He noticed the group of people approaching. His eyes stopped dancing and he stared.

'Come into the warm,' said Michael. 'We'll get you some dry clothes.' He took off his raincoat and offered it.

'You will never silence me,' he cried, hopping backwards on his one shod foot. 'Never.'

'What do we do now?' asked Dave.

'I'll call for backup,' said Brian, taking out his phone. 'And an ambulance.'

'So do you think he's the real one or the impersonator?' asked Michael, when Brian's call was over.

'It's hard to say. I hope he's not the real one though, for legal reasons.'

'Legal reasons?'

'Oh, er, there'll be less paperwork if he's the one we're looking for, that's all.'

'So we'll just keep an eye on him until help arrives,' said Michael. 'He should be OK. They say that lightning never strikes in the same place tw—'

Another bolt lit up the world around them and they watched in horror as flesh became transparent, revealing the clear outline of a skeleton. Before their dazzled eyes had a chance to adjust, they heard a voice. 'By standing on one foot, my life was saved. I tell you, science saved me.'

Michael felt his phone throb in his trouser pocket. Instinctively he took it out and looked at it. Through the puddles of light he could see that it was a message from the new Catherine. It read: *Merry Christmas, Michael xxxxx*.

'There is no God,' cried the voice from the darkness. A siren's wail harmonised with the howling wind. 'There is no God.'

Acknowledgements

I'm impatient to acknowledge my debt to the following people and things, real and imagined: Gilbert & Sullivan, Thomas & Lee, Parker & Stone, Purcell & Dryden, Linehan & Mathews, *Viz*, Gail Force, Talbot Rothwell, Greg Kettle, Francis Plug, Captain Adorable, Ben Hatch, *Spitting Image*, Mr Salteena, Tama Janowitz, Graham Lister, Bob Servant, the Stantons, *A Bic for Her*, Simon Crump, King Lear, Katy Guest, *The Gum Thief*, *A Night of 1000 Jay Astons*, Christopher Smart, Lionel Nimrod, Spinal Tap, Ann Teak, my long-suffering family and, above all, Mrs Slocombe.

Major thanks are due to everybody who supported the home-made first edition of this book, and who stuck up for the Prof and I through the year of struggle. Scott, Jane and everybody else at the Aardvark Bureau skyscraper deserve medals for not cowering under their desks, as does Alexander Tomský of Leda in the Czech Republic. And thanks to all at Conville & Walsh, particularly my indefatigable agent, Sophie Lambert.

Not everybody is as bright as you, and I have been advised to reiterate that this is fiction: it didn't really happen. Sorry about that. And even though you saw it coming from a mile away, please don't give away the ending. Thank you.

About the Typeface

Caslon is a long-running serif font first designed by William Caslon in 1722 and used extensively throughout the British Empire in the early eighteenth century. It was used widely in the early days of the American Colonies and was the font used for the US Declaration of Independence, but fell out of favour soon after. It has been revived at various times since then, in particular during the British Arts and Crafts movement, and again each time it went through a redesign for technological changes. It continues to be a standard in typography to this day.